FISHERMEN
OF KÉRITY

FISHERMEN OF KÉRITY

PETER JAMES QUIRK

WILDSIDE PRESS

Dedicated to my wife Elizabeth, who has read these pages so many times she could probably quote the entire book verbatim. Also to Carla Coupe my editor at Wildside whose invaluable observations steered me toward the completion. And also to my friend the artist Peter Keitel for painting his conception of Fishermen of Kérity; a fictional painting that features prominently in both the story and the cover.

PROLOGUE

Kérity, France—July 1940
A fishing village on the Atlantic Coast
during the Nazi Occupation of World War II

SS Oberleutnant Klaus Weber turned his motorcycle into the courtyard of a small farmstead on the outskirts of Kérity—the tiny Breton fishing village that was now his responsibility. It was also under his complete domination. Weber pulled up his motorcycle outside the modest farmhouse of Padrig Le Bras, a local fisherman and raconteur, and came face to face with the true reason for his visit. Jacqueline de Bavière—distant and haughty—would be his.

"Bonjour, Mademoiselle. Where are you going, and what is in your bag?"

She stared at him, eyes wide. In disbelief? Or perhaps guilt?

"Why are you bothering me? You know I am in mourning," she said, as she hastily pulled off her rucksack and threw it on the ground behind her.

Weber kicked his bike onto its stand, dismounted, and walked toward her.

"Give me that bag," he said, holding out his hand.

"This bag, it's nothing," she replied, breathing hard. "It's just a few treats for the Le Goff children. Food is hard to come by these days."

"You and I both know who that food is for. It's for that little Jew-boy—the son of Goldfeldt, that scum you took to your bed." He stepped closer. "Where is he?"

Jacqueline's eyes filled with tears.

Weber grasped her arms and held her firmly. Her breasts gently rose and fell under her peasant's smock, arousing him further.

"There is only one thing," he said, speaking softly into her ear, "that would make me forget the little Jew-boy you're hiding.

Starting this very minute, Jacqueline, you will become my woman to do with as I please. Do I make myself absolutely clear?"

* * * *

Four days later on the next farm, an armada of Nazi military vehicles streamed into Alain Le Goff's farmyard. Two motorcycles came first, then a chauffeured black Mercedes carrying two officers, followed by a truck with a dozen soldiers in the back. The convoy halted in the center of the farmyard, the soldiers leaping from the truck and forming a menacing line in front of the farmhouse door.

Madame Le Goff immediately called the children into the farmhouse, while Alain confronted the line of soldiers.

"To what do I owe this dubious honor," he said to the officer stepping from the Mercedes.

"I am in no mood for humor, Monsieur Le Goff," the officer replied. "Our commanding officer is missing. We believe the last person to see him was a Frenchwoman named Jacqueline de Bavière. She has stayed in your cottage. Where is she?"

"She comes and goes, Herr Leutnant," said Alain. "I don't remember seeing her today, but I'm sure she didn't even know your commanding officer."

As they spoke, the soldiers herded Alain Le Goff's family to the front step of the farmhouse. His wife and the three younger children, including five-year-old Fernand huddled beside the door, while his twelve-year-old twin sons were marched to the barn and pushed roughly against a side wall.

"According to my information, Monsieur Le Goff, this Jacqueline not only knew Oberleutnant Weber, she was his lover. We need to find her immediately."

Alain's only answer was a smile of disbelief. The Leutnant unholstered his Luger and held it against Alain's head. "This is no joke, Monsieur Le Goff. Where is she?"

As several soldiers aimed their rifles at the twins, Alain's wife screamed, gathered her younger children and pushed them protectively behind her. Alain tried to turn toward her, but the Luger's barrel pressed harder.

"I will ask you one more time, Monsieur Le Goff."

"For the love of God, Herr Leutnant! I haven't seen her in days," cried Alain.

Without turning his head, the officer called, "Shoot the boy on the left." He paused and said, "Think again, Monsieur Le Goff. Think again."

A short volley of rifle fire, and Alain dropped to his knees. "Have mercy, Herr Leutnant! Have mercy. The boys are only twelve."

"It is not I who is killing them, Monsieur Le Goff. It is you. You do not answer my simple question." He pressed the pistol against Alain's temple and raised his arm. "*Where is she?*"

Alain's head bowed, and the officer dropped his arm. Another rifle burst echoed through the morning air.

"Bring the woman to me," commanded the officer. When Jeanne-Marie stood before him, weeping, her gaze fixed on her kneeling husband, he continued, "So, Madame, I hope you are more intelligent than your husband. Otherwise, you will become a widow. Where is Jacqueline de Bavière?"

Jeanne-Marie Le Goff could not answer. She could only kneel, clasp her hands together and beg for mercy. A single gunshot was her reply.

The soldiers climbed back into their vehicles, and the armada drove out of the farmyard and down the dusty road.

1

Tommy Kiernan
Kérity, France—May 1959

A taxi pulled up beside the harbor, and the driver peered out of his side window and pulled a face. "Are you sure this is where you want to go? There won't be anyone around in this weather."

"Isn't this Kérity Harbor?"

"*Oui, Monsieur*, this is it."

"Then this is exactly where I want to be."

"Well, if you need to find somebody or want to get any questions answered, you might try that bar over there, L'Etoile du Nord. That's where all the fishermen go."

I paid the driver, thanked him and turned the collar of my pea jacket up around my ears, pulled the brim of my cap down closer to my eyes and stepped out into the wind and the rain. It was awful out there, but what did I expect? Nothing had gone right in my life for two years now. This rude awakening and the shock to my teen-age vibes began when my father—no, that's no longer correct—when the man I believed was my father walked out of my life, and culminated with the incomprehensible murder of my beloved mother. Did I expect the sun to shine on me now? No man, let the rain fall, let the wind howl. It suits my mood.

I walked over to the quay and studied the harbor. And although I'd never before seen it, it was like returning to a familiar neighborhood. I'd lived for years with my mother's painting of this same harbor hanging on her studio wall. *Fishermen of Kérity* she called it, and she would never sell it.

I'd also been born in Brixham, a celebrated fishing village on the South Coast of England, and that made all fishing villages seem familiar. Of course, when my mother painted her picture, the weather was much nicer than today, but there was nothing I could do about that. Everything had been nicer before. I now live under a dark cloud.

As I walked out along the sea wall, the rain eased a little. And by the time I reached the end and looked out over the vast Atlantic Ocean, the rain had slowed to a drizzle. The wind, however, was still driving huge waves into the harbor entrance, smashing them against the sea wall and then sending the churning remnants of the white caps across the harbor to die by the quay.

With raindrops and seawater dripping off the peak of my cap, I stood there. I had come across the Atlantic to meet a man. What would I say to him? A few weeks before I would have introduced myself as Francis Thomas Kiernan, Junior, but now I was simply Tommy. I still used the surname Kiernan because that was the name on my passport, but what my real name was, well, that was another of the reasons for my voyage to France.

I retraced my steps back along the sea wall and crossed the road to L'Etoile du Nord. This change had started a few months ago, on a near-fatal night back in Upstate New York, the night I began to suspect that perhaps my poor, innocent mother might not be quite as innocent as I believed—the night a stranger burned down my mother's house with us both asleep inside.

* * * *

Deep in the night, I woke suddenly coughing and choking. Something was terribly wrong. The room—my basement bedroom—was heavy with smoke. What was happening? I leapt out of bed and ran out of my room. I found myself staring at a shadowy figure who introduced himself by punching me in the face. I fell back against the bedroom doorway, but by using the doorframe as a launching pad, I sprang head first at the bastard. Maybe I could knock him groggy, or at the very least break his nose. But that plan didn't work. He saw me coming and stepped aside. And as I crashed into my father's old tool bench, he grabbed a large wrench from a wall hook and swung it at me. The wrench bounced off my head and dropped me to my knees. Then he threw it at me, and it bounced once again off the back of my head. He ran out through a side door.

I staggered, my head pounding. Yellow tongues of flame licked at my legs. My mother. Upstairs, still asleep. I had to get to her.

Step by painful step, however, I made my way upstairs. Smoke hung so low that by the time I reached her door, I was crawling along the carpet. I carefully opened her door—I didn't want the fire to flare up—and called out, but she didn't hear me. I leaned across her bed and shook her shoulder. "Ma!" I cried. "Wake up! We've got to get out of here."

Nothing. No movement… no noise…. Just silence. Was I too late? I hung my head. A moment later my mother began to cough, and I shouted with relief.

She opened her eyes briefly, and I scooped her up and placed her on her feet beside the bed. Her legs buckled. I wrapped her arm around my shoulders and half carried, half dragged her out the room, down the stairs and out the front door. I vaguely remember laying her carefully on the front lawn just as fire trucks pulled up, sirens blaring. I collapsed beside her.

* * * *

I opened my eyes. Where was I? *Who was I?*

I could barely move, and a dull, aching throb pounded at the back of my head. I lay still, waiting for my eyes to focus. When they did, I stared at a pristine white ceiling. Someone called out "Nurse!"

A hospital? But what was I doing in a hospital?

A vaguely familiar woman's voice spoke: "He's awake, Deputy. His eyes are open." A sympathetic face hovered over me. "How do you feel, Tommy?" she said, as I closed my eyes once again.

"Mr. Kiernan," said a deep, rumbling voice. "I am Deputy Perkins from the Greene County Sheriff's Department. Do you feel well enough to answer a few questions?"

I groaned. "Where the hell am I?" I hardly recognized my own voice.

"You are at the Albany Medical Center," he said. "Last night your mother's house burned to the ground, and you received a severe blow to your head. Do you remember anything?"

I tried to think. "My mother! Is she safe?"

The woman answered. Of course, now I recognized her voice. She was my father's Irish girlfriend, Annie.

"Jacqueline is down the hall in another ward; your dad and her friend Genna are sitting with her, but she's gonna be okay—thanks to you. You pulled her out of the house in time."

I tried to pay attention, but I drifted off again.

* * * *

A nurse stood beside me with a breakfast tray.

"How do you feel, Tommy?" she asked cheerfully, as she plumped my pillows and helped me sit up. "Would you like some orange juice?"

I reached for it gratefully. My mouth was extremely dry.

I took a sip. "Is the deputy still here?" I turned my sore head slowly.

"That was yesterday, Tommy. But he said he'd be back around ten this morning. Are you feeling strong enough to speak with him?"

"I think so…. But I don't know what I can tell him. I don't remember a thing."

After I swallowed the juice and ate a few mouthfuls of pancakes with syrup, I lay back down and closed my eyes. What had happened?

The only thing I could vaguely remember was the day before the fire, when a young man had come to my mother's studio to see, as he put it, what we had for sale. "I understand that the artist here is French," he had said. "What is her name?"

"Jackie Kiernan," I'd replied. "My father is Irish," I added in response to his raised eyebrows. "Her French name was Jacqueline, but she goes by Jackie now."

He had nodded and pointed to a painting on the wall. "That's impressive. What is the subject?"

"It's the harbor of a French fishing village, I think my mother lived there before the war—it's not for sale, but if you like French landscapes, there are a few more in the back room. You can go back there and look through them if you'd like."

The young man had gone back and studied the pictures. "They are pretty good," he had said when he returned. "How much do they cost?"

"I'm not sure, but Jackie will be back soon. Can you wait?"

"I'm afraid not; I'm on my way to meet people for a hike."

"That's a shame. She may have given you a discount on your purchase. But I can't."

"In that case," he had replied, as he moved toward the door. "I guess I'll stop back another time. *Au revoir.*"

* * * *

At precisely ten o'clock, Deputy Perkins returned and stood beside my bed.

"Hi, Mr. Kiernan," he said, holding out his hand. "Or may I call you Tommy?" I nodded and shook his hand. "You're something of a hero, you know. You saved your mother's life."

I stared at him blankly and cautiously shook my aching head. "I did?"

"Yes. If you hadn't pulled her out of the house, she might have died from smoke inhalation. As it was, it was touch and go. Are you sure you don't remember anything?"

I frowned. "The last thing I remember is trying to sell a painting in my mother's studio…. Oh, wait a second…. I remember waking up coughing and smelling smoke…" I paused. It was so faint. "I remember running out into the basement," I continued slowly, "and feeling a presence, like someone was there. But after that everything's a blur."

"There is a wound in the back of your head. Do you remember how you got that?"

"No, sorry."

"It's very interesting that you felt somebody's presence. It is too soon to pinpoint the origin of the fire, but preliminary investigations point to arson, which by extension also means attempted murder. Do you or your mother have any enemies?"

"Me? No. I just graduated high school. Who would want me dead? But my mother?" I shrugged. "She keeps to herself. Doesn't open up."

"Doesn't open up? What do you mean by that?"

"She doesn't like talking about her early life. 'The past is the past' is one of her favorite sayings. It's a shame, because I would have loved to hear about her early adventures. She escaped the Nazi occupation of France by fleeing to England. She met my father there, and that's where I was born."

Deputy Perkins asked a lot more questions, few of which I could answer. He even wanted me to describe the young man who came to the art studio.

"Why?" I asked. "What does he have to do with anything?"

"It's something you remember, Tommy, so it may be significant."

"He was tall, slim and pleasant, and that's all I remember. Sorry. People come in and out of the studio all the time in the summer. Before him there was another young man with a French accent. He came in with several kids from a Jewish camp over in Hunter. They loved my mother's paintings."

Eventually, after I began nodding off again, he left after saying he would return the following day. I lay in bed, trying to make sense of the detective's line of questioning. Somebody tried to murder my mother and me. But who? And why?

I closed my eyes and thought about my parents and our arrival in America.

* * * *

My Irish father, Francis Thomas Kiernan, Frank to his friends, was stocky, rugged with a love for the sea. And when he moved to England to take advantage of the wartime economy, he first worked for a fishing fleet, and because that wasn't tough or dangerous enough, during the darkest days of the war, sailed with North Atlantic convoys, where he was dumped into the ocean from two ships torpedoed by U-boats.

When he came ashore during the post-war building boom, he was known for his willingness to take on all kinds of back-breaking labor. Other work, he said, were jobs for toffs or poufters. A decent man when he wasn't drinking, all he really understood was the sweat and toil of jobs like tearing off roofs or digging ditches.

My French mother was very different. To me she was a beautiful, delicate flower with blonde flowing hair. I loved her dearly, but always at a worshipful distance. After we moved to Greenville, in upstate New York, I could feel the cracks in their relationship. Mom bought an art studio in the nearby mountains and stayed there for days on end, and dad spent more time with his drinking buddies in the Irish enclave in East Durham.

And although these comings and goings confused me, I quickly learned not to ask questions. Dad loved my mother's Continental elegance and accent, and he accepted any explanation for her absences. Dad knew her retreat was for her art work. But he was a simple man with simple needs. And I guess he started to look around.

Annie Morrison was the only daughter of Big Jim Morrison, the proprietor of the Shamrock, Dad's preferred bar. Located in East Durham, it was several miles south of our home. And when Big Jim was brought down by lung cancer—his inevitable reward for a lifetime spent in smoky saloons, not to mention his own three-pack-a-day habit—Annie took over. Shortly after Big Jim's retirement, however, dad broke up a vicious knife fight in the bar. And blond, buxom Annie, seeing a chance to rid the Shamrock of its bucket-of-blood reputation, set her sights on him: first by employing him as a bouncer, and then when my mother was away in the mountains, offering him delights he was no longer receiving at home.

This hardly caused a ripple in our house at first. My mother seemed not to notice this new arrangement, and her absences for her painting projects became longer and more frequent. But when Big Jim passed on to that great Guinness dispensary in the sky, Annie became more possessive. After she promised to set my father up with his own construction business, he moved in with her, filed for divorce, and set up in back of The Shamrock Public House and Restaurant—to give it its full name.

It wasn't until my junior year in high school that I learned my mother was a reasonably successful artist, and her frequent absences were for her art projects. I never understood why she hid this from me. It stung, a little. But when I began to think about my future, my parents were both becoming—not wealthy, perhaps—but financially comfortable. Of course, my father still drank to excess, but he no longer had to pay for it.

When my high-school graduation came closer, my mother wanted me to go to college. My father, however, wanted me to join him in the construction business—and become a bouncer, too, I'm sure. I thought about taking that easy route, but I worked a few Saturdays with him tearing off roofs, and that changed my mind.

Life in construction was hard. College and the prospect of a white-collar future seemed much better.

* * * *

The nurse interrupted my thoughts.

"You have a visitor, Tommy." She held open the door. I opened my eyes to see my mother being wheeled in by a hospital orderly. She looked pale and tired. No wonder.

"I hear you received a crack on the head, darling boy. How do you feel?"

"I'll be okay, Ma, but how are you? And did you hear the fire could have been set on purpose? Somebody might have tried to murder us. Who would want to do that?"

She shrugged.

"Maybe someone from your past, someone from France?" I continued.

"That was twenty years ago. And besides, when I left France I was escaping Nazis, not my compatriots. I'm sure the police are mistaken." She waved her hand, as if dismissing the idea.

"Well, a ghost didn't hit me over the head," I insisted. "Oh, the deputy sheriff wants to interview the young man who came to the studio the other day—especially after I told him he might be French. Do you know who he might have been?"

"No. In any case he would have been a baby when I was living there." She paused and frowned. "Which painting was he interested in?"

"He looked at all of them, but he didn't really say."

A strange expression crept across my mother's face as she sat back in her wheelchair. Then her face hardened, and she refused to discuss the subject again.

* * * *

In the summer of 1958, my mother drove me to Vermont to begin my all-too-brief stint as a student at Middlebury College studying English and French literature, with a minor in French. French had been my first language—although my mother and I switched to English as soon as I began attending school—and I was happy to see how quickly it returned. I threw myself into my studies with a joy I never believed possible.

In my quiet moments, though, I couldn't forget that somebody out there wanted to harm my mother, and possibly me, too.

2

The cold, blustery March day began as a day of promise—I caught the eye of a girl, a fellow student. A dorm-mate and I were on our way across campus to our first assignments of the day, and as usual we went past the tennis courts and cut through the cemetery. And even though the hood of my parka was up around my head and ears from the wind, how could I not notice the extremely lovely girl kneeling beside a grave close to the path.

We exchanged smiles as I passed, and I made a mental note that she was someone I would love to meet—and as soon as possible. And when I arrived at my lecture hall and was told to report immediately to the Administrative office, I went back through the cemetery and bumped into her again at the entrance.

"Hello again," I said shyly. "It's too cold to be hanging around in a cemetery. In fact, if I had the time, I'd buy you a cup of hot chocolate."

"And if I had the time, I'd go with you gladly." She smiled sweetly and held out her hand. "I'm Adriana, Adriana Baker."

"Wow, your hands are like ice. Let me try to warm them for you," I said, as I began to rub them gently. "I'm Tommy Kiernan, and I'm so happy to meet you. I hope we can get together soon."

"I look forward to it, but now I have to run."

She looked me in the eye, smiled, and I swear she blew me a kiss, although I may be wrong about that. Maybe I hoped she blew me a kiss. But after she began hurrying off, she did stop for a second and wave back at me. I know I didn't imagine that.

I continued on to the Admin office right past the grave she'd been tending. And I was dumbfounded by what I saw. The headstone told me the deceased was an infant girl who had passed away some seventy years ago. That alone would have set my head spinning, but also, lying on the grave was a fresh bouquet of spring flowers arranged around a tiny teddy bear.

Thoughts of Adriana and her unusual mission that morning floated through my head until I arrived at the office and found Deputy Perkins waiting for me. After we shook hands and were ushered into an empty conference room, I sat down across from him.

"Why are you here, Detective? Do you have more information about the fire?"

Perkins frowned and coughed into his hand. He looked very uncomfortable.

"Tommy, it is my unfortunate duty to inform you that your mother was the victim of an accident. She was found in her car at the bottom of a ravine near Katterskill Falls."

For a moment I was dumbstruck and stared blankly at him.

"How?" I mumbled. "When?"

"We are not absolutely sure, Tommy. She was found yesterday morning, but she probably died sometime the evening before. There were no witnesses, unfortunately."

"Did she simply slide off an icy road?"

"Again, we can't be positive. She was on a very steep hill with hairpin bends."

"But she was a very careful driver. Are you sure she wasn't forced off the road?"

"There is not enough evidence to say for sure. And if there was another car involved, we have yet to find it. At this point I can only say that we *are* treating this incident as suspicious, as we would any fatal accident. I do not wish to intrude upon your grief, Tommy, but do you mind if I ask you a few more questions?"

I shook my head silently, still not able to wrap my head around this awful news.

"We have spoken with your father, Tommy. I gather he and your mother were separated." I nodded again, and the deputy glanced at his notes. "How long has your mother owned her studio?"

"She has owned it for several years, long before my parents separated. I think she simply loved the peace and beauty of the mountains."

The deputy continued with his questions for a few minutes then gave me his card, offered his condolences once again and left me to deal with my grief.

* * * *

I sat for a long time with my head buried in my hands. The thought of never again seeing my beautiful, vibrant mother alive was horrific. I remembered the French lullabies she sang to me when I was a child—the long walks we took together through the mountains, the bouquets of wild flowers I gathered for her and brought back to her studio, especially during those beautiful spring mornings.

What was I going to do now? I couldn't simply return to college as though nothing had happened. If some savage ran my poor mother off the road, it had to be the same bastard who set the fire— but who could it be? She had no enemies I knew of, although I realized she was secretive, especially about her early life. Again I asked myself: What was I going to do?

I thought about finishing the semester; it was paid for after all, and I would have at least had the chance to spend some time with Adriana. But then I knew I was in a race against time too—the killer could still be after me. It was time to go home and research my darling mother's life.

Before I left, however, I instructed my dorm mate to track down Adriana and give her my address and phone number—after the fire we moved to an apartment, also in Greenville. I needed something positive to cling to on that otherwise horrendous day.

3

My mother's studio was located in a tiny hamlet high in the mountains above Katterskill Falls. This meant the only road up there was past the ravine that took her life. And that morning a thick fog shrouding the mountainside gave me the shivers and a renewed sense of urgency. Closer to the summit my car pierced through the fog, and I found myself speeding into the sunlight, not wishing to waste another second before sorting through my mother's effects and unlocking the keys to her mysterious life and sudden death.

As I walked into her studio, which was about fifteen miles from our house, I was immediately struck by the magnificent seascape on the wall facing the door. Of course I had seen it a hundred times before, but without really taking it in. In the days following the fire, my anxiety for my mother had been altogether too fresh—too raw—for me to notice paintings.

Now I studied it with an overpowering sense of pride, and I wondered for the first time about my mother's legacy. Who owned her paintings now? And I know it sounds stupid, but I also wondered if I could still afford going to college.

The painting showed a tiny fishing harbor before sunset. The rays of the setting sun sparkled on the tips of waves across the sea from the horizon and in through the harbor entrance. I caught my breath at its beauty. But who were the men in the foreground? Why, I asked myself, now that it was too late, why was my head full of questions?

How had a beautiful French artist and a simple Irish seaman/laborer wound up together in war-torn England? And this painting, a French fishing village—what had it meant to her? With these mysteries searing through my mind, I began to search every inch of her studio.

Two hours later I discovered a false bottom in one of her desk drawers, and underneath it a college ruled notebook filled with sketches and notations in French in my mother's neat handwriting. At last, I thought with perhaps not quite joy, considering the circumstances, but with the utmost relief, I had found what appeared to be my mother's journal.

Would this give me some answers? I sat at the desk and flipped through the pages. The entries seemed random, although at the beginning they were dated, going back as far as prewar France and her teens.

Jacqueline de Bavière was the only child of a petit-bourgeois wine *négociant* who scorned her artistic talent and then disowned her when she left home to join an artists' colony on Brittany's Atlantic Coast.

Between the sketches of peasants, landscapes and fields of prehistoric stone menhirs and dolmen, I learned that she made ends meet by working for the local government teaching French to the local kids—children of Breton peasants and fishermen. She met and became friends with a Parisian journalist named Jean-Pierre and a Breton storyteller called Padrig, who she began working with: introducing him to his audience and then passing around the hat after his performances. She would also try to sell her paintings. There were sketches of the painting on the studio wall, which my mother named *Pêcheurs de Kérity*.

At that point the entries became less frequent and I assumed war had begun to heat up, and that keeping a journal was suddenly much less important than staying alive. But then an entry describing my mother's escape to England and meeting Dad was followed by another describing her confinement during the bombing and her fears and anxiety for her baby and her.

Could that last entry be correct? It was dated September 9, 1940, two days before my birth. I quickly turned back to the earlier one, which clearly and vividly described her escape from France. "I was carried across *La Manche* by heroic Breton fishermen on a pitch-black night in the early summer of 1940."

I closed the journal in sudden confusion. What did this mean? But even as I told myself I didn't understand—of course I did. *La Manche* (sleeve) was the French name for the English Channel, which meant that when my mother escaped to England from

German-occupied France, she was already six months pregnant with me. Again I mentally kicked myself for never demanding answers. Why, for instance, was I named for a man who clearly was not my father?

I turned back to the beginning and began reading again—this time with a pencil and paper. But apart from writing that she was becoming fond of the children she was teaching, which included the large brood of a peasant-farmer named Alain, and the teenage son of a fisherman named Jakez, there was not much mention of her private life. Although she did write that Padrig's stories touched her deeply, and she'd featured his likeness in *Pêcheurs de Kérity*.

Fishermen of Kérity, the wall painting I admired so much. Now I knew the name of one man, but which was Padrig the Storyteller? I went over and studied it again. There were two men in the painting: A young man standing in the foreground staring out to sea through the harbor entrance, and a man possibly in his forties sitting by their boat cleaning seaweed and debris from their fishing nets. Most likely they had just returned from a day on the ocean. But which one was Padrig? And if it were the younger man, was he my birth father? And where was this fishing village named Kérity?

The name itself didn't sound French, apart from the acute accent over the *e*. But I had learned that Breton was a Gaelic language, so perhaps it was a Gaelic word. Where, I wondered, could I find information about this?

I would have to travel there myself and track down this Padrig, the sooner the better—after all, who better than a raconteur, as my mother called him, to tell me the story of my mother's life? I had to go, even if, or especially if, he turned out to be my father. I returned to the desk and the journal with a renewed sense of purpose.

I didn't learn any more, even though I read the journal from cover to cover twice. There was no mention of the other man in the picture. Was it the fisherman Jakez, the Parisian journalist, the farmer Alain, or simply a local fisherman recruited as a model? And why did my mother have to escape to England? The journal didn't tell me what I needed to know. Perhaps they were all fighting Nazis, and my birth father had been captured or killed.

For a moment I began to fantasize. Maybe he was a legendary hero of the Résistance, and all I had to do was go to Paris, claim his heritage and his medals, and reap the glory of his fabled life and celebrated death. My delusions faded quickly—nothing was quite that simple or that heroic.

I looked at my watch. There was still plenty of time to go to East Durham and confront my father with the journal and its contents. This time I would not be stopped by half-hearted or evasive answers. I wanted the whole truth. Before I left, however, I called my dear mother's friend Genna, an art historian and appraiser, and asked her to meet me at the studio to discuss her paintings.

I then drove up to East Durham and down the winding road toward Annie's Shamrock Pub. Poor Dad. I was going to pretty much ambush him. But I needed answers.

4

When I entered the Shamrock, my father was tending bar and holding court with a few regulars, while Annie was sitting at her usual spot by the cash register in deep conversation with one of the wives.

"So," she said, giving me a sympathetic smile. "Our hero returns. What did you find?"

"Enough," I replied. "I can't discuss the details out here in the bar, but it looks as though I might have to go to France."

"What's that, son?" said my father, as he poured a pint of Guinness.

"I'll tell you in private, Dad, but I'm sorry to say, you're not going to like it."

"Why don't you two go into the office?" said Annie. "I'll hold the fort."

"So, son, what's the story?" said Frank, after he closed the door behind us.

"This, Dad, this is the story," I said, as I dropped my mother's journal on the table before him. "And you have a lot of explaining to do."

My father picked up the journal and flipped through the pages. "I can't read this," he said. "It's in bloody French."

"But you know what it is, don't you? You've seen it before, I'm sure."

Dad nodded. "Yes, it's your mother's journal. It's where she wrote down all the things she didn't want to discuss with me. And she wrote it in French just to piss me off."

"Did it never occur to you to learn the language? It might have helped your relationship."

"Learn French! Are you kidding me? Listen, Tommy, I grew up speaking Irish, and I was having a hard enough time learning and speaking English. Trying to learn French too would have made my head spin off my shoulders." He looked at me with a worried expression. "You must have read it by now, son. Tell me what you learned."

"What do you know about Mom's life in France, Dad?"

"Very little. She just told me she was involved with the Résistance, that her friends were killed by the Nazis, and she escaped just in time."

"Was her boyfriend killed, too?"

"Well, yeah, but I didn't hear about him until later. You see, we were staying in the same lodging house, and she was awful good to me. She cooked my meals and washed my clothes—we became very close very quickly, even though we couldn't communicate very well. I'd never met anyone so beautiful, and I would have done anything in the world for her."

"According to the journal, you pretty much did."

"What do you mean by that?"

"Didn't she ask you to marry her?"

With that, Dad's face crumpled, and he slouched down in his chair. "Did she write that in the book?"

"No, not exactly, but it does imply she was six months pregnant when she arrived in England. You must have known that."

"I didn't realize it at first; she was very thin. I was working on the boat that picked her up. We met with some French fishermen out in the Channel. It was a regular thing. Our captain worked for British Intelligence, and we used to exchange packages with the French once a week. Occasionally we would transfer couriers, too."

"Spies, you mean."

"Courier was the official name, but of course we all knew what they were. And most of them never returned, although that was never mentioned, either."

"So one night you picked up Jackie?"

"Not just Jackie. There were two of them, Jackie and a boy about ten. The Frenchies told us they were wanted by the German authorities, but they didn't explain why. That was enough for us, though. They were freezing cold, wet and miserable, so I gave them blankets and tried to warm them up. Jackie was so grateful, and by the time we got her back to Brixham, I was in love."

"What did you do?"

"There was a spare room at my lodging house, so I brought them home with me. And it would have worked out well, except that she and the boy didn't get along. They were always shouting at each other in French or another language, which I later learned was Breton. The fishermen in that part of France speak it. He was a little pain in the ass, that boy."

"What was his name?"

"Ephraim, although I didn't learn that right away. An interpreter came down from the Free French headquarters in London to question him. It turned out the kid was Jewish and his father had been killed. The interpreter took him to a Jewish orphanage in London. Your mother explained that Ephraim's father was arrested and killed by the Nazis and the kid thought it was her fault."

"What do you mean 'it was her fault?' Did he give a reason?"

"She told me that Ephraim was living a very secluded life, training to be a rabbi when the Nazis marched into Paris. He couldn't understand why his father took him away to Brittany, where there were no Jews and almost nobody even spoke basic French. It was a completely foreign world to him, and his first reactions were to rebel against everything and everybody."

"I wonder where he is now," I said, mainly to myself. "And does he still hate Mom?"

"All I know is after he was taken away," said Frank, "life got much better at the boarding house. I would bring food home and Jackie and I would cook together. She would even wash and mend my clothes, and in the evenings we would listen to the radio. We were probably the only people in the world who learned English listening to Churchill's speeches."

To prove his point Frank stood, raised his arm in the air and started quoting: "'We shall fight them on the beaches; we shall fight them in the streets... We shall never surrender.'" He smiled sheepishly. "It made sense at the time, and it made us feel safer. We became very pro-British as they battled the Nazis alone, and we learned to communicate in English and get to know each other."

Listening to my father talk about their courtship was very touching. He said that for a lonely Irish boy who came to England to find work in the wartime economy, meeting Jackie was the best thing that could have happened to him.

I could only imagine the security it brought them both during those terrible times. "So," I said, "when did you realize she was expecting a baby? That must have been quite a shock."

"Well, of course it was. But I was nineteen, very green, and still a virgin, so when a sophisticated Frenchwoman like Jackie took me to her bed I could hardly believe it. And from that moment on, one word from her, and this Tipperary peasant boy would have jumped off a cliff. You know what I mean, son, don't you? Or maybe you don't."

Frank gave me that knowing 'are you still a virgin, too?' look. I didn't respond, which I'm sure told him all he needed to know.

"So, anyway, one night she broke down in tears, and when I tried to comfort her, she told me she was pregnant. She said her boyfriend was betrayed to the Nazis and shot. But when she composed herself, she took me by the hand and asked me to marry her and adopt her baby as though it—you—were my very own. Well, what do you think I said? I couldn't refuse.

"You pretty much know the rest. And let's face it, I might not be educated, I might not be sophisticated, but I've been a decent father. You never went hungry, you slept in a dry bed—even if it was an air raid shelter—and we all survived the war. That was a miracle in itself."

"Dad, I'm not complaining about my life, I just wish I knew more about it sooner. I would have loved to hear about your life in Ireland or Mom's life in France. I think it would have given me more of a sense of family."

"But why do you want to go to France? Do you want to learn about your birth father?"

"That's one reason, Dad. But I also need to know if there is someone from her past who hated her enough to want to kill her. I mean, you've already given me the name of one possible suspect. Besides, do you remember the painting on Mom's studio wall? There were two men in the picture, a young man who might have been her boyfriend and an older man. This older man was mentioned in the journal. She called him Padrig the Raconteur, or storyteller."

"What kind of stories did he tell?"

"I don't know, but he might be just the man to tell me about Mom's life in France."

"But where would you find him? France is a big country."

"I have to do some research, but that painting on the studio wall is called *Fishermen of Kérity*. I've checked a map of France, and Kérity is a fishing village on the Atlantic coast in Brittany, and just across the English Channel from Brixham. So that's a good place to start. Most ocean liners go into Cherbourg, in Normandy—also very close to Brittany."

"Ocean liners are expensive as hell. These days you can find a cargo boat that carries a few passengers. They're a lot slower but also a lot cheaper, and if you find the right one, it might drop you off even closer to your final destination. You can contact the New York Harbor Master's office to get a list of the ships in port, when they leave and their final destinations. When were you thinking of leaving?"

"I don't know yet. I haven't thought it through. How much time do you think I need? And come to think of that, what about the family finances? Do we have the money for this trip? And do we have the money for me to continue my education?"

"I don't know. I know I don't have it. Everything I earn goes to pay off the money Annie loaned me to start my business. As for your mother, I have no idea where she kept her money. That is, if she had any to start with."

I clutched the sides of my head in despair. "All her records probably disappeared in the fire," I said. "But I guess I'll start asking around. But in the meantime, how long would it take me to earn enough to go to France working for you and Annie?"

Enlisting Frank's help would make it much easier than trying to do everything behind his back. But it turned out that he wasn't yet convinced.

"Why the hurry, Tommy? It's not as though you are going to change anything."

"Well, whoever burned down the house tried to kill me too, Dad, and he may try again. I also don't understand why Mom worked so hard to hide her real identity. To start with, she married you almost as soon as she got to England, and that changed her name. And then when I was born you named me Francis Thomas Kiernan, Jr., which moved her further away from her French past.

"And keep in mind that before the war she had already sold a couple of paintings as Jacqueline de Bavière, so when we came to

America and she started painting again, don't you think it strange that she didn't resume under her old name? She began again as Jackie Kiernan."

5

The following day I met with Genna DeGraw at my mother's art studio. Genna first came to the studio to put a value on a painting one of her clients was considering buying. And after falling in love with Jackie's work, they began working together and became friends. Genna was married to a reasonably successful author who was also a creative writing instructor at a community college. We didn't know each other well, but our meetings had always been positive. And as someone who was very low-key and a little shy, I admired her flamboyant personality and especially loved her sweetly dramatic entrances everywhere she went.

Today was no exception: "Hello, dear boy," she warbled, as she swept into the studio with what appeared to be a picnic basket and a bottle of wine. And after depositing them both on a nearby table, she gathered me up in her arms and pulled me into her ample bosom. "I miss your mother so much," she said. "How does one survive such an unspeakable tragedy? Jackie's passing is such a loss to our artistic community and to me personally. God only knows how you must feel."

I kissed her cheek and escaped from her grasp, "Thank you, Genna; I knew I could count on you." She took a couple of steps back and gazed sympathetically into my eyes.

"What are you going to do now that your life has been turned upside down?"

"That's one of the reasons I need to talk to you. How well did you know my mother, Genna? Specifically, what do you know about her finances?"

"Not a lot, my dear, but I did sell a couple of her paintings. Why do you ask?"

"Well, I don't know where she kept her money, and because our house burnt to the ground, I don't know where to look."

"Oh dear," she said, as she went over to her basket and changed the subject. "Are you hungry, I brought us some lunch? Do you have a refrigerator here?"

"Yes, there's a small one with a stove and a sink in the back."

"Well, pop that into the fridge, dear boy." Genna handed me the bottle of wine.

I read the label: "Alsatian Riesling, how nice," I said, trying to sound worldly and sophisticated.

"Of course," she said with a knowing smile. "All meetings go down better over a meal and a glass of wine, and there is nowhere in these mountains where you can buy a decent bottle with lunch." Genna shook out a red checkered cloth and spread it over the table and returned to the subject of finances. "Of course you need to find her money. How about your tuition? Is that paid up?"

"As far as I know it's paid until the end of the school year, but I don't know about next year. But I also need to go to France."

"Oh, how exciting! Where did that idea spring from?"

"Do you believe my mother was murdered, or do you think it was an accident?"

"I don't like to think that she was killed deliberately, but do you know something I don't? Here, take a slice of Quiche Lorraine."

"I don't know what to believe, but the police are labeling it suspicious, especially after someone burned our house to the ground last fall."

"But why do you want to go to France? Have you learned something troubling about your mother's past?" Genna's face expressed concern. "It has to be, Tommy. What have you found?"

"I was rooting around the studio searching for clues to my mother's life, and I found more than I bargained for, much more than I could even understand."

"What do you mean, darling boy? Although before you tell me, why don't you be a dear and open the wine?" I went back to the tiny fridge and brought the bottle back to the table, and Genna took a corkscrew from the basket and handed it to me.

"I'm not sure I know how to do that. I've never done it before."

"Then it's high time you learned, especially if you're planning a voyage to France. First, you use this tiny knife blade to cut around the foil over the cork." She watched me with an indulgent smile. "Great job," she said. "You're a natural; now you simply twist the corkscrew all the way into the cork and pull it out. *Voila!* Now pour the two glasses to a little less than half full, and you will be the complete French *bon vivant*."

As soon as I poured the wine, Genna lifted her glass. "A toast, Tommy; a toast to your dear, dear mother," and as I raised my glass, she continued: "God speed, Jacqueline, and may your spirit return to us each spring to brighten our mountain landscapes with your exquisite brush strokes and glorious splashes of color."

Her words moved me deeply and I reached over for Genna's other hand and gently held it as we touched our glasses together in somber tribute.

"Now, my dear, tell me what you found that troubled you so much."

"Did you know that my mother lived in England?"

"I suppose I did. Isn't that where she met your father?"

"Actually they met in the middle of the English Channel when she was escaping the Nazis, and she transferred from a French fishing boat to an English one. But that's not the shocking part. When she arrived in England, she was six months pregnant with me."

Genna suppressed a smile. "What a surprise! How did you learn all this? Did you find her diary?" Genna took a huge gulp of wine. "I can hardly believe it; such intrigue. Is there more?"

"Oh yes. She came to England with a Jewish boy she'd been hiding from the Nazis. But for some reason, he hated her and blamed her for his father's death."

"And all this was in her diary?"

"No, Dad told me some of it when I confronted him with the fact that I knew he wasn't my father."

"So I guess you want to go to France to sort out all this amazing information. Would you pour me another glass please, dear boy?"

I poured the wine as I answered: "Yes, but first I have to find the money."

"Ah, money," she said. "I don't believe you need to worry about money. The paintings here are quite valuable, especially that one on the wall." She nodded over her shoulder to *Fishermen of Kérity*. "And it's a sad fact that when an artist dies, his or her works usually double in value."

"What are you suggesting?"

"Well, if you trust me enough to make me the official executor of her artistic property, I will write you a check for five thousand dollars, which you can return to me at a later date or sell me one of her paintings, and in which case, the check would serve as a down payment. In the meantime, however, you can make your mysterious voyage to France, and when you return, you can continue your education."

6

Padrig Le Bras, Fisherman and Raconteur
Kérity, France—May 1959

A stiff west wind and the foaming white-caps running before it foretold a long and difficult day for those who clawed their living from the sea. But of course *Kenavo* sailed out; Yann had a reputation to protect. We all knew Yann Le Corr didn't cower in the harbor for anything less than a tempest of biblical proportions, peg-leg be damned. I went with him for a simple, more practical, reason—I needed the money.

But now our catch was in and our nets cleaned and stowed—the day, a good one, as it turned out, was finally over. I called to Yann, who was standing at the edge of the jetty scowling at the sea as he would a vanquished foe. And as he turned to answer me, he spat into a wave as it exploded under his feet—a gesture of defiance I knew only too well. My partner—a happy and curious boy when first I knew him—had become increasingly bitter and antagonistic since his father and I brought his broken body home from the war. It grieved me to watch him struggle with his demons, but how many times could I remind him to forget the past? Nothing would ever bring back his leg.

Our end-of-day handshake was a salute to solidarity—we had fought the elements together and beaten them. But then I turned away. Enough was enough. I had a life to live, and that life craved conversation and laughter. Climbing onto my bicycle I pedaled straight to the harbor tavern, L'Étoile du Nord.

I had hardly entered the building, however, when Amélie, the barmaid and owner's daughter, called to a young man seated at a table.

"This is Padrig Le Bras, Monsieur." She then turned to me. "Padrig, this young gentleman would like to meet you."

I turned toward the stranger in anticipation and watched him walk purposefully across the bar. He was a tall young man, possibly not even twenty, but he had an air of quiet confidence. Was he perhaps a journalist? There had been a time when journalists and writers sought me out for tales and anecdotes of Breton peasant life. He seemed a little young for that, although there was something about him—I knew not what—that recalled those happier, pre-war days.

"Monsieur Le Bras," he said, as he came toward me hand outstretched. "I am honored to meet you. And if you are not too tired from your grueling day, I would like to buy you a drink, and perhaps ask a question or two."

I nodded politely, and when he steered me to an alcove by the window, I sat across from him and studied this strangely familiar person anew.

"Have we met before?" I said, even as I struggled to identify his accent—his French, though reasonably accurate, was quite rusty.

"No, Monsieur," he said. "But you knew my mother."

At that moment, Amélie brought me my cider, which I gratefully sipped while I digested this information. "I'm sorry," I said. "I am at a loss. You say I knew your mother?"

"Yes, Monsieur, she is, or was, the artist Jackie Kiernan, although when she studied art here in the late thirties, her name was Jacqueline de Bavière."

The mention of Jacqueline's name startled me, and the young man noticed it immediately.

"I'm sorry if I alarmed you," he said, studying me carefully. "Please allow me to introduce myself and explain why I am here."

"I owe you that much," I said, as I raised my glass.

"My name is Tommy Kiernan and I was born in England—my parents met there during World War II—and we immigrated as a family to the United States some eight years ago."

Sadness crept into his voice as he continued. "Just recently my parents separated, although financially they both seemed to be prospering. My father owns a construction business, and my mother was selling her paintings. Then, back in the early spring, somehow her car slid down a ravine in the mountains. She was killed instantly."

"I am sorry for your loss," I murmured. "But what brings you here to me?"

"When I was sifting through my mother's possessions at her art studio, I came across an unfinished journal, written in French. And now after translating it for my father and learning much more about my mother than I ever before knew, I have come to France to try to find a reason for her premature death."

"But wasn't it an accident?"

The boy shook his head. "We do not know for sure. I learned later there were tire marks on the road that didn't match her car. And several months before her death an arsonist who was never apprehended set fire to our house at night while my mother and I were asleep inside. That is why I made the journey here. I'm searching for a hint, a clue that might help me to understand why anyone might want to kill my beautiful and loving mother—a woman who, I'm sure, has never hurt anyone in her life."

"And your father, how is he taking this?"

"He is mourning her loss, although they had separated before she died. He fully supported my journey here."

"And what exactly do you want from me, Monsieur?"

"Please call me Tommy, Monsieur."

"Then you must call me Padrig, but again I must ask what brings you here to Kérity, and specifically to me?"

"You are mentioned in my mother's journal. She considered you her friend, and she admired your storytelling skills. But also, she had a favorite painting, a painting she would never sell; it is entitled *Fishermen of Kérity*, and it is the only work of hers that hangs like an icon on her studio wall. This painting depicts two men cleaning their nets at sunset on that jetty over there." Tommy nodded out the window toward the sea wall. "And one of those men looks remarkably like a younger version of yourself."

He reached into his pocket, pulled out a photograph and pushed it across the table.

I studied the picture and realized immediately why Tommy seemed so familiar: If he believed that the seated man resembled a younger me, had he also noticed the one standing in the foreground was a slightly older incarnation of himself?

"It's very lovely," I said. "When was it painted?"

"I was going to ask you the same thing. Have you not seen it before?"

I shook my head. I was not yet ready to answer questions.

"Look, Padrig, I came here to trace my mother's journey through Brittany, and according to her journal, you worked part-time entertaining guests at the local *auberge*. She wrote that you were a raconteur with a prodigious memory for Breton folk tales and legends. Surely you of all people can provide the information I need."

I drained my drink and considered my options. The news of Jacqueline's death effectively relieved me from my oath of silence, but did I really want to tell her son the sordid truth? Perhaps the best solution would be to let it die along with his mother.

"It was a long time ago, Tommy," I said. "And I haven't been commissioned to tell a story in years."

"Are you sure there isn't something you know that would tell me more about my mother?"

He paused and searched my face for a reaction, but I was still conflicted. I rose to my feet.

"Jacqueline fled France under an extremely dark cloud," I replied, "a cloud that also enveloped those who befriended her."

The young man held up his hand. "Please, Padrig—Monsieur Le Bras," his tone became more urgent. "That was some twenty years ago, and now she is dead; there cannot possibly be any repercussions at this late date. Besides, you say you haven't been paid to tell a story in a long time. Well, we have had *Fishermen of Kérity* and several more of my mother's paintings appraised, and they are very marketable. I am prepared to offer you ten percent of the current value of *Fishermen of Kérity* to learn of my mother's life in Brittany, and also how and why she left for England so abruptly."

He turned toward the bar, called for more drinks, and then pulled a checkbook from his breast pocket. "I am going to write a check payable to you for ten thousand francs. And if I'm satisfied at the end of the evening that your story is credible, I will sign it. You will receive the remainder of the money when the facts can be corroborated." He opened his checkbook and began to write.

Amélie arrived with our drinks, and I returned to my seat. This meeting had suddenly become something my peasant soul understood very well—this young man was going to pay, and pay handsomely, to listen to a story.

I sipped my cider then leaned back in my chair to collect my thoughts and allow my long-dormant alter-ego to step to the fore. I was no longer an anonymous peasant fisherman; it was the thirties once more, and I was Padrig the Breton, entertainer and raconteur *par excellence*.

7

It was 1939, in early spring, I believe. Yes—it was April—not long before the declaration of war. During those uncertain times, life in the region continued as always—shelter and food being the principal concerns of Breton peasants. Of course we discussed the news and the prospect of war, even though we also knew full well we were in no position to do anything about it. At the time, I worked part-time as a raconteur of folklore and stories of life here in *La Bretagne*. And I had been retained to entertain guests at the Auberge du Pont, an old inn and tavern on the outskirts of Kérity, on Saturday evenings.

My journey to the Auberge took me along footpaths and over the styles and fields of this land where my forebears have toiled shoulder to shoulder since man has walked upon this earth. Above me the evening sky was studded with stars, and the air around me brimmed with the scents, sounds and promise of the upcoming season. And I remember being inspired, as I so often was, to capture in my tales the rugged beauty of the earth beneath my feet and of the wild sea that surrounds us, shapes our souls, and perfumes every breath we take.

Please forgive the florid language, Tommy, but deep beneath this rough peasant smock there beats the heart and soul of a poet. I had an arrangement with the innkeeper. He would provide me with a meal when I arrived and top up my glass occasionally during the course of the evening. In return I would entertain his guests with tales and stories of folklore and legend culled from all walks of Breton life—sailors, fishermen, farmhands, priests—and all corners of the land. And at the end of the evening, when I ended my program, the innkeeper would see to it that someone, if possible an attractive young lady, would come forward to thank me for my stories and take up a collection on my behalf.

That evening Jacqueline de Bavière was in the audience, and it was she who the inn keeper prevailed upon to lead the applause and pass the hat. I knew her vaguely, she worked in the neighborhood teaching French to my Breton neighbor's children, and she had been sitting at a table in the back of the room with some friends. With blond hair and green eyes, she was very striking—the sort of woman who stood out in a crowd. She was dressed casually in the bohemian style of the day, as were her companions, and I wasn't surprised to learn they were members of an artists' colony that lived and worked in and around Pont Aven, whose beautiful vistas and landscapes had been made famous in the late nineteenth century by Paul Gauguin.

Normally before I began my program, I would take some time to get to know my audience, and then I would tell the stories I believed would please them. If it was an audience of a certain age, perhaps on a pilgrimage to a *pardon* or to some other religious site, for example, I would tell stories of saints and abbots and other icons—there are many from which to choose.

But this was a younger, more boisterous crowd, and I began the evening with a tale of death and disaster on the high seas:

"*Bonsoir, Messieurs, 'Dames.* Welcome to Brittany and welcome, on this beautiful spring evening, to the Auberge du Pont. I hope you all enjoyed your dinner tonight—I know I did. There is nothing like the taste of wild boar fresh from the Black Mountains, washed down with a fine bottle of Muscadet from our vineyards on the banks of the mighty Loire. Have you replenished your glasses? Yes? Then, with your permission, I shall begin.

"Tonight I'm going to take you back two hundred years and out onto the Atlantic Ocean during the storms of November. And to give you an idea of how we feel about this time of year in Brittany, I just have to tell you that the term for November in our native Breton is *Du* or *le mois noir*—the black month.

"There are three men fishing off the Iles de Glénan this night in November. Their captain, Gildas, a seaman with the strength and endurance of five ordinary men, is rowing, and his two companions are paying out the nets. It is high tide on the Atlantic Ocean, and a storm is gathering to the west. The wind is picking up and the waves make it difficult to keep the boat on course. The men are silent—they know the danger, but they have families to feed, and besides, they have nearly finished securing the nets. Soon they can turn back to harbor, back to their *chaumières* where their wives and children crouch anxiously by the hearth praying for their safe return.

"There is the deafening roar of thunder, and the turbulent waves light up as though it were day as a hundred lightning bolts rake the skies. The boat is knocked sideways by a huge wave, and the three men grasp the boat's gunwales quickly as another wave sweeps away their oars. Then, as the skies darken once more yet another mountain of water breaks over the tiny boat and the three men are tossed into the teeth of the storm.

"With their captain leading the way the ill-starred fishermen begin to swim towards the nearest island using the lights from a distant cottage as their beacon. Somehow, the wild tides bring them close to the shore, and Gildas helps each man fight through the surf and onto the beach. He carries them up beyond the high-water mark, and finally, with his shipmates lying prostrate on the shore, he turns back to the raging sea to try to salvage his boat, the sole source of his livelihood. But this was a doomed venture, even for the mighty Gildas—and not only was he never seen again, but his body was never recovered.

"But, since that dreadful night, it is said, any fishing boat in trouble near those fateful islands during the storms of the Black Month is guided back to harbor by the ghost of Gildas. Some men even swear they have seen him swimming through the churning seas pulling their boat to safety behind him. Others say that Gildas comes to them in their dreams to warn them of an upcoming gale or to advise them where schools of fish might be on that day and where to cast their nets.

"And now, *Messieurs, 'Dames*, I would like you to raise your glasses to Gildas, that he might continue to watch over and protect the fishermen who ply their trade on the wild and treacherous seas that surround us here in Brittany."

After a round of applause, I told a couple more tales, and at the end of my performance, I held my hands up to the crowd and bowed deeply in all directions. And moments later, Jacqueline jumped up, grabbed my cap and began a collection. She went from table to table—smiling, teasing, cajoling—and refusing to budge until everyone had contributed something. When she presented me with my money, I was standing at the bar deep in conversation with a writer from Paris.

The writer, whose name was Jean-Pierre Goldfeldt, had many questions concerning my tales, but when Jacqueline joined us and we stood there drinking and chatting, I watched his focus change gradually from Breton legends to this blond artist with the green, laughing eyes.

Before I left the inn that night, however, they both wanted to know where they could find me again—Jacqueline because she thought she might depict one of my stories in a painting, and Jean-Pierre because he wanted to gather material for an anthology of Breton tales and legends.

8

Two months later, in June, the Parisian writer walked onto my farmstead one morning while I was feeding livestock. He reintroduced himself, and then, perhaps because he realized he was intruding, that it was not the time or the place to be discussing stories, he pulled off his jacket, rolled up his sleeves and enquired if there were anything he could do to assist.

At first I was skeptical of this writer whose hands had never held a shovel nor pulled a rope, but he seemed instinctively to know what I needed. He took the measure of the property in a single, sweeping glance, then picked up a pail, walked over to the well, and began filling the water troughs in the pigsties.

We worked side by side without speaking. But we accomplished a great deal, and I was grudgingly impressed by his enthusiasm. He saved me so much time in fact, in the afternoon we were able to replace the hinges on a shed door, a task I had been avoiding.

But when we had finished and stowed away the tools, he stood hesitantly in the yard, momentarily unsure of what to do or say.

I gave him an opening. "Would you like something to eat?" Relief was visible on his face as he smiled and nodded. "Follow me," I said, and I brought him into my cottage, offered him a chair by the window and cut up some bread, cheese and fresh tomatoes and set them on the table. Then I took an earthenware pitcher and went out to the barn to draw some cider.

Jean-Pierre collapsed gratefully onto a chair, and he didn't utter a word until he had finished eating. He then sipped his cider and pulled a silver cigarette case from his pocket. Flipping open the lid, he placed it on the table between us.

"Would you like one?" he asked.

I wasn't really sure. In those days you didn't see tailor-made cigarettes very often, especially deep in the countryside where everyone I knew rolled his own from a tin of tobacco and cigarette papers. Of course, I had tried them once or twice but didn't really like them. However, it was something for nothing and that's hard to turn down. My frown changed to a grudging smile as I nodded my thanks.

Jean-Pierre struck a match against the underside of the table and we both lit up. Then he leaned back in his chair with a long sigh and discharged a thin stream of blue smoke up over his head.

"You know, Padrig," he said, "I've only been in Brittany a few times, but it's beginning to grow on me. It's beautiful out here."

"It's okay if you don't mind hard work," I replied. "But, is it Brittany you like or is it that blond artist you met at the Auberge du Pont? What was her name again?"

"Jacqueline."

"Ah, yes, Jacqueline."

"Maybe it's a little of both," he admitted sheepishly. "I've just broken up with my wife."

"You left your wife for Jacqueline?" I said, shaking my head in amazement. "Wasn't that a little foolhardy?"

It seemed to me that a writer with a wife in Paris could have a quiet fling in Brittany without anyone being the wiser. But perhaps city dwellers lived by a different set of rules.

"No, no," he said. "That's not it at all. I did leave my wife, but it had nothing to do with Jacqueline. We'd been fighting for years—ever since our son was born. My wife comes from a very religious family, you see—her father's a rabbi, and I'm more of a secular Jew, if you know what I mean."

Unfortunately I had no idea what he meant, but I wasn't going to admit that to a Paris intellectual, even if he could find his way around a farm. I just nodded my head wisely and hoped the meaning would become evident during our subsequent conversation.

"For years I've been talking about quitting my job and writing a novel," he continued, "but my wife always discouraged me. She said I was being irresponsible. When I met you at the *auberge*, it came to me that an anthology of Breton folklore would be a much easier sell, especially for an unknown author. But when I broached the subject to my wife, she had a fit and said if I went off to Brittany chasing legends, I needn't bother returning.

"Well, I thought it over for a week or two. Then, one night I went home and announced that I had taken a leave of absence from my job. For her, that was the last straw, and as I expected, she asked me to leave. So, here I am with very little money, no job, no family, and no home."

"You can always join the army," I said, referring to the war rumors and recruitment posters that seemed to be everywhere.

"Yeah, I know," he replied, shaking his head. "But if we do go to war, I promised my boss I would go back to the newspaper and work as a war correspondent. I know the signs are pointing that way. What do you think, Padrig?"

I shrugged. "I don't know what to believe. All politicians are liars."

Jean-Pierre nodded in agreement and then changed the subject: "You don't know where I can find a place to stay, do you?"

I thought for a moment. "There's a small farm down the road from here," I said, slowly, "with a tiny cottage in the back. The farmer's parents used to live there, but the father died a couple of years ago, and his mother died last Christmas. It's been empty since then. I'm sure you could have it for the summer by working off the rent on the farm. Alain can always use an extra pair of hands."

Jean-Pierre's eyes opened wide. "That would be perfect. When can I go and see him?"

"He'll be at the market on Saturday. You can speak with him then."

"But what will I do until Saturday?"

I glanced out the window at the setting sun then looked him up and down. He had an honest face, even if he was 'secular,' whatever that meant, so I made a quick decision.

"Listen, Jean-Pierre. I have to leave—it will be low tide shortly, and I have to go to Kérity Harbor to bring in my trammel nets. I'll be gone for the evening, so if you want you can make yourself at home here. There's a spare *gwele klos* in the parlor, you can park yourself in there for a night or two."

"A what?"

"A *gwele klos*—come, I'll show you." I brought him into the other room and pointed. "Those cabinets there—against the wall," I said. "You'll find them in every household in the region. You have to understand, Jean-Pierre, we're a poor people with small homes and large families, so we sleep in these self-contained beds with sliding doors. Once you climb inside and close the doors, it's like having your own room. I've slept in one my entire life."

Jean-Pierre looked skeptical, so I opened a door, revealing the mattress and bedding.

"Trust me," I said. "It's quite comfortable."

"Okay, Padrig. When in Rome, I guess. I'll give it a try. Thank you." He still looked a little doubtful, but then his expression changed. "What's a trammel?" he asked.

"It's a type of fishing net. It's a way of catching fish without having to be there, if you know what I mean."

His face twisted into a puzzled frown until he saw me grinning. "*Touché!*" he said, smiling. "You're a busy man, Padrig," he continued. "You run this little farmstead; you make cider and sell it; you're a well-known storyteller and entertainer, and now you tell me you're a part-time fisherman. What the hell else do you do?"

When I didn't answer immediately, he shrugged it off.

"Never mind," he said. "We'll talk about that another time. Tell me about trammeling. How does that work?"

Jean-Pierre's questions were beginning to tire me. "Are you going to pay me for all this information?"

"Of course you will reap the benefits when I publish my book. You are going to have to trust me until then."

"I thought as much," I said, with a resigned sigh. "Trammel nets are employed to catch fish using the ebb and flow of the ocean tides. You wait until two hours after high tide—that's when most of the seaweed and debris flows out—then two men take the nets out in a boat and set them in the sea adjacent to the shore. At each end of these nets there's a rope with an anchor holding down the bottom and a float holding up the top—and one man rows more or less parallel to the shoreline while the other pays the trammel nets out into the sea. At low tide, you pull them in—hopefully loaded with fish. Then all you have to do is clean the nets and sell the catch."

He pulled out a notebook and began writing furiously. "How long are the nets?" he asked.

"It depends on the weather. On a normal day we set about fifty meters of nets; but if it's really calm we can usually put out more. Of course, if there's a gale or a storm we don't go out."

"It sounds really easy."

"No, not at all," I replied, shaking my head at his naïveté. "There are two tides every day, and you've got to go out at high tide and low tide. And when you're not on the water, you have to clean and repair the nets, sell the fish and look after the boats. It's a lot of work, especially if you do it full-time. I just help out when I can."

"What sort of fish do you catch?"

"Flatfish mostly: flounder, plaice, Dover sole…" I glanced again at the setting sun. "Listen, I've got to get going. Make yourself at home; I'll see you in the morning."

"Can I come with you sometime? I want to learn everything I can about peasant life."

"I don't see why not. I'll talk to the men that own the boat. They're a father and son, Jakez and Yann. But I think it'll be okay. There are times when it's difficult to find two people to go out at every tide. We've all got other jobs. But if you're willing to learn the ropes and take your turn from time to time, that would help a lot. There's one problem, though; Jakez doesn't speak French."

"I'm going to have to learn how to communicate in Breton. I think Jacqueline speaks it more or less fluently. This will give me an excuse to contact her again," he said with a smile. "I'll ask her to give me a few lessons."

9

Daybreak would usually find me on the porch behind the cottage. There on an old wooden bench I would roll a cigarette, sip my coffee and ponder the upcoming day. And as I mapped out my workload, any potential problems were muted by the scent of lilacs and by birdsong that floated in from the oak sentinels that lined the unpaved road.

That morning was no exception, and I was lost in thought when a noise in the kitchen reminded me I had company. Moments later Jean-Pierre rounded the corner with a steaming mug in one hand, a slice of bread in the other and a shock of unruly black hair tumbling across his eyes.

He stopped for a moment while he breathed in a lungful of fresh morning air, sat down on a step and sipped his coffee. Then, swiping the hair from his eyes, he turned to me with an amused grimace: "*Sacré bleu*, Padrig," he said. "Is this black crap supposed to be coffee, or did I pour myself a mug of tractor oil by mistake?"

"That's how I like it," I grunted. "But there's some goat's milk in an urn under the sink if you need to cut it down."

He shook his head. "Nah, I'll get used to it," he said. "What can I do for you this morning? When do you have to go fishing again?"

I wasn't accustomed to discussing my daily life with anyone, much less answering a barrage of questions first thing in the morning. But Jean-Pierre had an easy, friendly manner, and I found myself explaining the workings of my small farmstead and listing the upcoming chores; he, in turn, shared his ideas for his volume of Breton tales and legends.

He also talked me into taking him on my next fishing expedition.

* * * *

We went down to Kérity harbor in the late afternoon. And as we walked across the wharf, Jakez waited for us at the top of the steps leading down to the water. He was sitting on a stone bollard, his broad back hunched forward and his black cap jammed down over iron gray hair. Deep in conversation with a friend, his huge hands stabbed at the air as he punctuated his speech.

"Jakez," I said, after the other man had turned back to his tasks. "This is Jean-Pierre. He's a writer from Paris. He wants to learn all he can about the Breton way of life, including fishing. I told him he could come out with us this evening. Is that okay?"

Jakez looked him up and down disdainfully. "Does he speak Breton?" he asked.

I shook my head. "But he's a good worker," I replied. "He's been helping me on the farm. You'll see."

"*Bonjour*, Jakez," said Jean-Pierre, proffering his hand. "*Comment allez-vous?*"

At first, Jakez ignored him and began to move toward the top of the steps. But then with an apparent change of heart he spun back around, grasped the outstretched hand, nodded and grunted.

Then he turned to me: "Padrig, you two carry the gear down to the end of the pier. I'll go and bring in the boat."

I nodded to Jakez and smiled at Jean-Pierre. "Congratulations, you've been accepted for now," I said in French. "Come with me and try not to screw up. Above all, don't get in anybody's way when we're hauling in the nets."

That evening we were retrieving the nets that Jakez and his son had set earlier in the day. Consequently, we didn't need much equipment: just the outboard motor and a can of gas. To my surprise, despite the language barrier, Jean-Pierre's lack of experience, and Jakez's native mistrust of strangers, the Parisian writer held his own. He had a great curiosity and an eagerness to learn, and his attention to detail with even the most menial of tasks had our skipper nodding his grudging approval. For someone who was unaccustomed either to sailing or hard physical labor, he passed his initial test with flying colors.

After the boat was back in its berth and the nets were cleaned and stowed away, we walked across the harbor for a drink.

Jakez ordered a round and turned to me: "Your friend did well tonight," he said. "He can take a shift or two if he wants.

Of course, he'll have to work with you or Yann because he only speaks French, but if that's okay with you, I can live with it."

"Thank you, Jakez," I said. "I'm sure that's what he wants. As a team we can cover the evening tides during the week, since I'm busy most weekends with the market and the *auberge*. But maybe he can come down on Saturday afternoon and help clean the nets or take the catch to market."

Jakez nodded and then changed the subject: "What's the latest news from Paris? Ask him what they're doing to prevent a war."

Jean-Pierre, who had been making notes in his journal, lifted his eyes when he heard the word 'Paris' and gave me a quizzical glance. I repeated the question.

He looked at Jakez, smiled ruefully and shook his head. "Not very much," he replied. "The French and British governments are being much too soft, and Hitler's taking full advantage. It seems to me he's doing everything he can to get a war started. Last year he swallowed up Austria; this year he sent his troops into Czechoslovakia—and nobody lifted a finger.

"Now he's threatening Poland, and thanks to the Treaty of Versailles there's no way Britain and France can let that slide. But there are people in Paris who actually admire the bastard. And that's madness—especially with all the stories coming out of Germany about the way he's treating Jews."

I translated his answer, and Jakez took it all in with a grim look on his face. "I don't think Bretons want to go to war over a bunch of Jews," he said. "Most of us—and that includes me—have never even met one."

"Well, Jakez," I replied, "you've met one now. Jean-Pierre is Jewish. Do you want me to tell him what you just said?"

"You can tell him whatever you damn-well please. I spent four years on the Western Front in the last war. My brother and my best friend died for nothing, and I don't want to lose my son because Hitler doesn't like Jews."

Jean-Pierre had been trying to follow the conversation, and when he caught my eye, he asked what Jakez had said.

"He's worried about his son," I replied. "If there's a war, he'd be one of the first to go."

"Yeah, I can understand that. But he said something about Jews. What was that all about?"

Reluctantly, I translated his remarks, adding my own comments: "You have to understand, Jean-Pierre, family means everything to us here in Brittany. That's all we have."

He looked at Jakez and nodded his head slowly. "Tell him I understand him completely," he said. "But I think we all have to face up to reality. There's going to be a war."

10

During the next few weeks, Jean-Pierre Goldfeldt became, to all intents and purposes, the first and only Jewish Breton peasant. He moved into the cottage down the road and worked off his rent in his landlord's fields. He also helped on my farm in exchange for my stories and made a little pocket money fishing with Jakez. On Saturday evenings he would come to the *auberge*, or wherever I was appearing, and listen to my tales, and when he wasn't fulfilling his other obligations, he would shut himself in his cottage with his writing. Or so I thought.

We had just returned from fishing, had set the nets after a high tide, and he invited me into his cottage for a drink. It was a warm, hazy Sunday afternoon. And when we jumped down from our bicycles and turned through a cut in the yellow gorse that led to his cottage, I was amazed to find a young woman sunning herself outside the door.

She jumped up to greet us.

"Hello, Mr. Le Bras," she said, in Breton. "How do you do? I'm Jacqueline de Bavière. You remember me, don't you? We met at the Auberge du Pont, and we spoke after your presentation. It's nice to see you again."

"Jacqueline! Of course I remember you. How could I not?" I said. "But I'm not the local squire, you know, I'm just a peasant who works all the hours the Lord provides to keep the wolf from the door. Please, call me Padrig."

"You're much too modest," she replied, beguiling me with her smile. "You forget I've been part of your audience; I've seen you in action. When you weave your stories, you hold your audience in the palm of your hand. You mesmerize them. You're not just a peasant, Padrig. You are a troubadour—a true poet of the Breton soil."

"No, no," I protested, although much flattered by her words. "My evenings at the *auberge*, I must admit, can be rewarding. But when all is said and done, it's just another means of putting food on the table. But you—your work—to be able to take a scene, a slice of life, and capture it on canvas for all eternity… that—that is art." I threw my hands in the air in wonder at the suggestion that I, a mere teller of tales, could compare with that.

"Do you have a project in progress at the moment?" I asked, as she linked her arm in mine and guided me gently into the house.

"No. I've just finished one," she replied. "Now I'm searching for something new—something out of the ordinary. Jean-Pierre suggested a seascape. He thinks the harbor at Kérity would make the perfect backdrop. So, I'm here on a reconnaissance mission. You'll stay for a bite to eat, I hope? Supper's nearly ready."

Sitting around the kitchen table with Jean-Pierre, we reverted to French, and Jacqueline revealed that she had already seen the harbor and was excited by the possibilities.

"Of course," she continued, "the sun sinking into the Atlantic behind the lighthouse would be lovely. But that's a little trite—any hack could come up with that scene. I like to put a little action into my work. You know—some people—in this case fishermen. In fact, I would love it if you and Jean-Pierre would model for me."

"I don't know about that," I said, shaking my head slowly. "It's not that I don't want to help you, but it would take too much time. I don't have the time to stand around the harbor posing like a Parisian pimp while you paint me."

"We've already discussed that," Jean-Pierre interjected. "And I suggested that perhaps we could be repairing the nets after a day at sea. You know—sitting on the wharf with the harbor and its boats all around us, and the ocean stretching out in the background. We spend a lot of time doing that, anyway, and we don't move around very much. So that might work, and it wouldn't waste much of our time."

While I was mulling that over, Jacqueline continued to plead her case: "You would only have to be there for the preliminary sketches, of course. Most of the actual painting I would do in the studio."

After supper, and after I had conceded, Jean-Pierre refilled our wine glasses and suggested that we step outside.

"Come," he said. "Let us share this Breton sunset that inspires us in our separate artistic endeavors."

When we were settled in our seats, I turned to Jacqueline beside me and watched as she sipped her wine, leaned back in her chair and gazed dreamily off into the sunset.

"So, Padrig," she said, without turning her head, "when is the tide going to cooperate with my plans?"

"In two weeks, the low tide will begin to move toward the middle of the afternoon," I replied. "Then we would spend the evenings cleaning nets. The tides are a half hour later every day, so that would give you at least two hours each evening for a week. Would that be sufficient?"

"Perfect," she said, as she leaned over and kissed my cheek.

We spent another half hour with our wine and conversation before I reluctantly stood up to leave. There was something captivating about her presence, and as I cycled back to my farm, I began to question my decision to remain single, and I found myself wishing I were Jean-Pierre—even if it was just one night.

11

On September 3, 1939, Hitler's armies marched into Poland, and our peasant lives as we knew them ceased to exist. I remember sitting in Jean-Pierre's cottage listening to the radio when Great Britain and France declared war on Germany.

We looked at each other with solemn faces, and my friend shook his head in disgust. "That's the end of my book of Breton legends, I guess," he said. "I've got to get back to Paris."

He was gone by the end of the week. And then the following week Yann joined a regiment that was forming at Vannes, and after a short period of training he was sent to Verdun to guard the border. Like a good son he wrote home every week, and Jakez showed me his letters when we went fishing.

Jean-Pierre also wrote to me several times. His editor sent him to Strasbourg so he could monitor the German frontier for any action that might unfold. But by the following spring, when Rommel's Panzer divisions began rolling into Luxembourg and Belgium, I lost track of him, although I assumed he was now moving with the army.

Soon after that I ran into Jacqueline at the market, who told me he was back in Paris.

* * * *

Over the next few weeks, my neighbor Alain and I listened in horror and disbelief to Jean-Pierre's radio as the whole Western Front collapsed, and our once proud army scattered and fell back in disarray. The single bright spot that whole spring was the evacuation of the entire British Expeditionary Force, along with 80,000 French soldiers, by the British Navy. They were snatched off the beaches at Dunkirk against terrible odds, while the Luftwaffe strafed them from the skies, and the rear guard fought off the Wehrmacht.

It had been, of course, a complete and utter defeat, but just the fact that so many men were saved—picked up and spirited across the Channel to England—was, to us, a miracle.

Meanwhile the French Government fled from Paris to Tours and then to Bordeaux, then Daladier resigned and Pétain stepped in. He moved the Government to Vichy, sued for an Armistice with Germany and broke off relations with Great Britain.

In retaliation, Britain recognized General De Gaulle as the head of the Free French, and De Gaulle launched his famous radio appeal on June 18th—"France has lost a battle, not a war…"

Pétain condemned him to death immediately and signed an Armistice with Hitler.

Two weeks after the Germans arrived at the gates of Paris, they marched into Quimper, the nearest large town to my farm, and the Breton people, angry and confused, braced themselves for Nazi occupation. As far as the official French government was concerned the war was over, and over the next few weeks Breton soldiers, who had marched off so proudly just weeks before, began to straggle back to the region in twos and threes—filthy, hungry and exhausted.

* * * *

A frenzied banging from without brought me to my feet. A soaking rain had been falling for hours, and I half-expected to find a patrol of bedraggled German soldiers on my doorstep seeking shelter. But when I pulled back the door, there was Jakez, water streaming from tattered oilskins and a look of desperation etched on his anguished face.

"What has happened to our boys?" he cried. "There has been no news. The airwaves are dead. What are we to think? What can we do?"

I quickly brought him in the house and helped pull off his oil-skins. There was nothing to say or to ask, his face told me everything I needed to know. I poured him a cognac and waited.

He took several gulps of the fiery liquid, then set down the glass.

"I sailed down to Vannes yesterday and went to my son's regimental headquarters, but a German army unit has already taken over. Most of his fellow soldiers come from that area, so I walked around the harbor asking questions. But no one knows anything; none of the men are back yet. I don't know what to think."

"It's too early to worry," I said, without conviction. "It's unlikely the entire regiment was captured. But Jakez, look at the bright side; perhaps he was rescued at Dunkirk, and now he's sitting in some English pub drinking beer. How could he get word to you from there?"

The possibility of Yann being in England brightened Jakez's mood considerably, and I promised to monitor the Free French broadcasts from the radio at Jean-Pierre's cottage.

But when he came looking for me several days later and found me with Jacqueline listening to a broadcast, it was he who had the news: "Some men from his regiment are back," he said, excitedly. "One of them brought a message to me. My son is alive!"

"That's great news," I said. "Where is he? Is he a prisoner?"

"No, but he was wounded; he took a bullet in the leg. His friends carried him as far as Nantes, and now he's hiding at a doctor's house getting treatment. I have the address. We just have to go find him and bring him home."

"And just how do you propose we do that? We can't just go and fetch him on the train; he's a wounded soldier. The Germans would simply pick him up and send him off to prison camp, and we'd probably be put up against the nearest wall and shot."

"No, Padrig. Not the train—the boat. We'll go get him with the boat. They can't stop us fishing. We'll sail down the coast, and if we see a German patrol boat, we'll just throw our nets into the water."

"You think we can just sail down to Nantes in an eighteen-foot sailing dinghy in the middle of a war!" I said, shaking my head. "Have you thought it through?"

Jakez nodded his head vigorously. "Sure," he said. "It'll be easy. Those *Boches* aren't so smart. They lost the last war, didn't they?"

"You have to go, Padrig," said Jacqueline. "Yann is a wonderful young man. You have to help save him."

I was silent for a few minutes. Jakez hadn't even asked if I was willing to go with him. He just assumed that, as a member of his crew and an old friend, I would do whatever he wanted—sail into hell, if need be. But I guess he was right. I had known him since the First War, and I'd watched Yann grow up, fished alongside him since he was seven. If Yann needed me to help save his son—how could I refuse? It was just a matter of how and when.

"It's going to take at least five days to get to Nantes and back," I mused, almost to myself. "That means I have to ask Alain to feed my livestock." I looked at Yann: "Are they issuing fishing permits yet? We're going to need some form of identification. There will be patrol boats everywhere."

"Come down to the harbor as soon as you can," he replied. "I'll take care of the permits. Oh, and when you talk to Alain, don't tell him any more than you have to. He can't tell the Nazis what he doesn't know."

I looked up sharply. "Don't you trust him?"

"We don't know who to trust yet," he replied. "The war has only just arrived here. Nobody has had time to choose sides. Just don't tell him anything he doesn't need to know."

I walked with Jakez to Alain's farmhouse. But when I stopped beside the gate and turned toward him, he grasped my wrists, his face choked with emotion.

"Listen, Padrig. I… I… This means everything to me… he's my only son… Mother of God, you know what I'm trying to say."

Then his arms dropped to his sides, his face softened as he nodded his thanks. He turned on his heel and continued on his way.

When the door to Alain's house opened, an eight-year-old girl stood before me, a solemn expression on her face and a finger held to her lips:

"Shhh," she whispered. "Poppa and Momma are listening to the Free French broadcast from England. We have to be quiet."

I smiled grimly. Alain and his wife, Jeanne-Marie, had five children, and I could only imagine what dire threats it took to keep them all quiet for fifteen minutes. I walked in and was waved to a seat.

"De Gaulle's calling for massive resistance against the invader," said Jeanne-Marie. "Whatever we can do—anything from civil disobedience to armed insurrection. But it's hopeless. What can we do? What would happen to the children if we were killed or sent to prison?"

I realized then that Jakez was correct. Everyone's priorities were different, and until they committed to the cause you couldn't say a word, and especially not in front of children.

I stood and motioned to her husband.

"Alain," I said. "I was going to ask you something, but I realize you have your hands full. I'll be over at Jean-Pierre's cottage with Jacqueline. We're listening to the radio, too. Keep up your spirits."

When I walked back to the cottage, Jacqueline's mood was markedly different to that of her neighbors. She leapt out of her chair and ran to my arms:

"Oh, Padrig," she cried. "France, our beautiful homeland—there are no words to describe how I feel. The sight of these strangers—these Nazi soldiers—marching on the sacred soil of our ancestors makes my skin crawl. For my family in the east this is the second time in twenty-five years. What can we do? The pigs are everywhere!"

I held her closely as I tried to console her. "I know, Jacqueline, I know," I said, softly. "But we have to be patient. We can't be hasty and do something stupid that gets us shot in the first week of the occupation. We have to sit back and size up the situation. And when we know who our allies are, then perhaps we can do something."

I pulled away from her gently, and she stood there, her body heaving with silent sobs.

"Listen carefully, Jacqueline," I said, as she wiped her eyes. "There is something you can do. Will you feed my livestock while I go with Jakez?"

She studied my face carefully and nodded her head. "Be safe, my friend, and God speed to you both on your journey." Then her features hardened again. "Have you heard from Jean-Pierre?"

The question took me by surprise. "Not since the invasion. Is he still in Paris?"

"I don't know; I haven't heard from him either, and I'm getting worried. I hear they've been rounding up Jews and deporting them to labor camps in Germany."

"Jean-Pierre is well aware of that," I replied. "He's not just going walk up to them and surrender. If he has no other option, he'll make his way back to Brittany. Trust me, Jacqueline. Here he can melt into the landscape as a Breton peasant, and if he learns to speak Breton, he can pretend he doesn't speak French. At that point he can hide out indefinitely, working the land or fishing with Jakez."

* * * *

The next morning, while riding to the harbor, I was dragged from my bicycle and searched by an enemy patrol just outside Kérity. On that cloudless summer day, I received an abrupt demonstration of the weight and the consequences of Nazi occupation. We Breton peasants were still struggling against the abuses of the landowners and their minions 150 years after the revolution, and my body convulsed in silent rage as I watched any gains we might have made goose-step away in gray uniforms.

I met Jakez on the wharf and he brought me up to date: "A company of *Boches* marched into town yesterday. They bivouacked in the schoolhouse and took over the village hall."

"Is it complete chaos?"

"No. I stopped by there this morning; it's really not that bad. Luckily for us they kept the village secretary, and she told me they would be issuing fishing permits tomorrow. We have to get one for the boat, and one for each crewmember. But there's a catch. Each man has to go down to the hall and get his own."

"Can't she give us an extra pass for Yann?"

"She said that each pass has to be stamped individually by the officer in charge. There's no way around it."

I cursed them roundly and spat on the ground. However, those very acts of frustration gave me the seeds of an idea, and I told Jakez I would work on a solution that evening and meet him outside the hall in the morning. Then I rode back to my farm and spent the remainder of the day showing Jacqueline around the property.

In the evening over dinner, I explained our new situation and the dilemma we faced. She was receptive, even enthusiastic to my rough-hewn plan and offered some suggestions. But the next day outside Kérity Village Hall she was not so sure.

"How do I look?" she asked for the tenth time. She was wearing Jean-Pierre's wool sweater and oilskins, an old pair of clogs, and her long, flowing hair was crammed up into my navy-blue fishing cap.

"You look great," I said, reassuringly. "It's as though we just brought in the nets. But remember, when we get inside, stand behind Jakez and pretend you don't speak French. I'll do all the talking."

"Don't you think the secretary… What's her name again? Anna? Don't you think that Anna doesn't know who he is? Won't she realize we're trying to fool her?"

"You don't have to worry about Anna," I replied. "She knows Yann's away in the army. But she can't ask the Germans for three passes if there are only two men standing by her desk."

"And I just stand there looking dumb?"

"No, not dumb, simply inconspicuous. You're a fisherman who suddenly needs a pass so he can continue to make his living. Believe me, Jacqueline, we'll be in and out of there in no time—the quicker the better."

Jacqueline was silent for a moment, then she smiled and nodded. "Okay," she said. "Let's get it done before these damn clogs cripple me permanently."

12

The following day, we sat in the harbor café with perhaps twenty other fishermen, waiting for the morning tide to turn. Jakez sat across the table from me, jaw set and tight-lipped, hunched over his coffee. One could only speculate what was on his mind as we prepared to sail into the unknown. I, on the other hand, tried not to think about it, and I contemplated the room, listening to fragments of conversation.

"Are they going to search our boats?"

"Do you have your permit?"

Just two months earlier these men would have been animated and good-natured, as they discussed the weather, the price of fish, their families. But now, they were confused, angry and resentful—the Nazi jackboot had suddenly become a cruel reality in their daily lives.

ACHTUNG! screamed a notice on the cafe door—a warning to a vanquished people that for every German soldier found assassinated, ten civilians would be selected, taken to the nearest wall and shot.

But out in the harbor, Jakez's boat the *Kenavo* was ready, straining against her moorings, impatient to be underway—to take a stand—to show these strutting peacocks that if taking our land had been easy, holding onto it was going to be a long, treacherous ride.

Jakez glanced at the wall clock. The morning tide had begun to ebb and soon dozens of boats would be pulling out of the harbor and heading for their secret fishing grounds. We wanted to be part of that exodus.

"Okay," he said, finally. "It's time." He nodded toward the other men as they gathered their equipment and headed for the door.

Once outside the cafe, I heaved my duffel onto my shoulder and crossed the road to the jetty where the crowd had stalled at the top of the stone steps. Barring the way was a German sergeant armed to the teeth and bolstered by a squad of infantrymen standing off to his left.

"You must show me your identity cards," he called in halting French, in response to any and all questions posed.

I eased toward the front of the crowd to watch the drama unfold. The sergeant's expression was tense, and so were those of his men. The fishermen, however, were beginning to enjoy his inability to speak Breton and were making no attempt to respond in French. They didn't realize the gravity of the situation and that they could be shot at any time for no apparent reason. Even Jakez had a smirk on his lips.

I dug an elbow into his ribs. "Jakez," I warned, "he's losing his patience. If we aren't careful, someone's going to get hurt."

Jakez quickly came to his senses. "You're right," he said. "Those *Boches* look ready to start shooting. You'd better see what you can do."

I nodded, took a deep breath and stepped out in front of the crowd. "*Guten Morgen, mein Herr,*" I said, using my entire German vocabulary to draw his attention.

To my surprise, his demeanor relaxed immediately, and that reassured his men, too. Behind me I could hear Jakez calming the fishermen, and I was reminded of the awesome powers of reason and diplomacy.

I held out my arms in a vague gesture of appeasement, and continued: "No, Sergeant, I don't speak German but, unlike my compatriots, I do speak passable French. Would you like me to act as your interpreter?"

He was as relieved as I was to break the tension, and it wasn't long before everyone had received the Third Reich's authorization to pursue the only livelihood they had ever known. Mine was the last ID to be returned and, with his task complete, the German sergeant came over to thank me for my assistance. There was an uncomfortable pause, after which he held out his hand.

What was I to do? Ignore the outstretched hand and risk being shot? Or did I shake it and face the wrath of my friends, my compatriots?

Once again, diplomacy saved the day: "Listen, Sergeant," I said, quietly. "I was glad to help you back there. I don't want to see decent family men getting shot for little or no reason. But for all that, we are still on opposing sides, and I hope you will forgive me if I don't shake your hand. I'm still going to be living here long after you've gone home."

"I quite understand," he replied. "I'm not a career soldier, either. I, too, would prefer to be back with my wife, my family and my friends. Good luck with your fishing."

With that, the offending hand became a wave, and the sergeant turned back to his men.

* * * *

Once we cleared the harbor entrance, we raised the sail and made for the open sea. "Take her out a ways," called Jakez, after he had scanned the horizon, "then steer a course for the Iles de Glénan. We need to stay away from the mainland as much as possible."

"If we island-hop all the way down the coast we should stay out of trouble," I agreed.

Jakez nodded grimly. "The *Boches* have only just got here. They couldn't possibly have had time to establish control of every community. The smaller islands probably aren't even occupied yet. There must be fifty of them in the Gulf of Morbihan alone." His eyes swept the skyline one more time. "At least the weather's good; if it stays like this, we can keep going all night."

That seemed a tad optimistic to me. "I don't know about that," I countered. "The *Boches* are not stupid. If they see a boat they don't recognize sailing down the coast in the middle of the night, they would probably blow it out of the water just for target practice—especially when we get near the big naval bases like Lorient or St. Nazaire."

Jakez's face tightened; he didn't like unsolicited advice. But he relented a little and shared his thoughts: "I know we can't do much about St. Nazaire," he replied. "It's on the mouth of the river. But we can stay away from Lorient. We'll head for Groix. I want to sail into one of the tiny fishing harbors there and look around. You never know, we may learn something we can use later."

The island of Groix, which was located just west of the entrance to Lorient harbor, was well visible from the mainland. But it was far enough away, we hoped, that we wouldn't excite any patrol boats. That was the theory. But as we sailed farther down the coast it became apparent that the venerable old seaport, laid out by Colbert in the Seventeenth Century, figured quite prominently in German naval strategy. There was much activity, both in and out of the estuary.

We were still some three leagues away from Groix when we had our first shipboard encounter with the enemy. A gunboat came roaring out of Lorient and bore down on us at high speed. At first, we feared she was going to plow right into us, but at the last moment she veered to starboard and cut her engines. She circled around us several times as she slowed, while her grinning captain and crew inspected us for weapons. And when the gunboat finally pulled in beside us, the captain leaned over from the bridge, lifted a megaphone to his lips and called out in Teutonic French:

"Ahoy there, *Kenavo*! Where are you from and what is your business?"

Jakez, who was livid from the near collision, shrugged his shoulders and pointed to the fishing nets: "Drop dead, you useless pile of dogshit," he called back in Breton. We both smiled and waved.

Plainly puzzled, the captain frowned and pointed to our name. "What does *Kenavo* mean?"

"*Au revoir*," I replied. "We're fishermen out of Kérity, just west of here."

"Do you know you need a permit to be out here?"

I nodded and patted my breast pocket. Apparently this and the fact that we were clearly non-threatening seemed to satisfy him. He nodded back, lowered his megaphone, and barked an order in German. The gunboat pulled away and headed back to Lorient.

I turned to my companion. "That was pretty stupid. If he had understood what you said, we'd both be dead by now."

"There aren't many Frenchmen who speak Breton. Where the hell would they find a *Boche* who speaks it?"

"Listen, I'm here because I want to help you bring your boy home. I don't want to die because you can't hide your feelings. There are lots of things we can do to get rid of these pigs, but shouting insults at them in Breton is just useless bravado."

Jakez's response was a scornful expression and a loud snort. He then busied himself raising the sail.

I grasped the tiller and turned the boat back into the wind, and once more we set out toward Groix. We knew that on the leeward side of the island there were several tiny fishing harbors we could enter. In one of those, we hoped, we could get something to eat and drink, and maybe rest up for the night without causing too much commotion.

* * * *

Toward the end of the second day the *Kenavo* entered the Loire River estuary and sailed past the provisional German fortifications at St. Nazaire without arousing any overt curiosity. We continued upstream toward Nantes through river traffic, which, surprisingly, was quite heavy despite the recent incursion, and I suggested to my captain that we should perhaps take advantage of our engine.

By way of response, Jakez, who had been sitting in the bow studying the buoys and landmarks and comparing them to his dog-eared river chart, got to his feet and began lowering the sheet. He came aft to help me to lift our outboard over the stern and clamp it down. Then he stowed the canvas while I primed the pump and began coaxing the motor into action. After a few wheezes and sputters we were under way again, and it was not long before the spires, towers and jetties of Nantes came into focus off the starboard bow.

"Shall we just pull in, make fast to a pier and ask for directions?" said Jakez, as he studied the shoreline. "I'm not all that familiar with Nantes."

"We don't have much choice," I replied, with a shrug. "But let's continue upstream and make note of likely moorings. And when we come about, we can tie up at the most promising one."

About an hour later I cut the motor and we drifted in beside a run-down jetty. And after securing our lines to metal bollards, we climbed back on board to eat the last of our provisions.

"Do you know where we are, exactly?" asked Jakez, as he reached for the cider jug.

I shook my head. "I've only been here once or twice. Let's head into town."

"I don't think we should leave the boat unguarded," he replied. "You don't need me with you."

While that was certainly true, there wasn't much that an un-armed Breton fisherman, who spoke neither French nor German, could do to protect the boat, either. But I wasn't about to remind him, given his recent outbursts; so I kept my thoughts to myself and prepared to disembark.

At that moment, the roar of an engine brought us to our feet. We scoured the waterfront as a motorcycle and sidecar turned onto the dock from between two abandoned warehouses. It roared up to the jetty, and the soldier astride the machine—a splendidly attired cavalryman replete with helmet, jodhpurs and black-leather gai-ters—dismounted and unclipped a sub-machine gun from beneath the handlebars. He held it loosely but kept it aimed in our general direction as the man in the sidecar, a ranking officer, stepped out and pulled himself erect beside him.

"Don't do or say anything stupid," I warned my volatile com-panion. "Our story rings true. I just need to stay alive long enough to tell it."

At that moment, the officer, a major, called out in fluent French: "Step down from the boat, put your hands on your heads, and then walk toward us slowly."

As we climbed down to the dock and my back was turned to the Nazis, I whispered nervously to my companion: "Be really careful, Jakez. This guy speaks very good French."

"Where are you from and what is your business?" demanded the major as we approached.

We stopped momentarily, and I shook off my funk as though it were stage fright. I pretended I was back at the *auberge* in front of an audience: "We are Breton fishermen, Herr Major," I said, lower-ing my hands slowly. "We sail out of Kérity, which lies north-west of Nantes, near the Pointe de Penmarche."

"Ahh, yes," he interjected in Breton, "that's Bigouden country, is it not? I know that region rather well. I used to spend summers with a family near Quimper when I was a student."

My face must have telegraphed my amazement, because he laughed out loud as he continued: "You're a long way from home. What brings you to Nantes?"

"Herr Major, one of our crew was badly hurt in an accident at sea last week. We brought him to Nantes and left him with a doc-tor. Now we have come to take him home."

His eyes narrowed as he pondered our circumstance. Then he ordered his man to lower his weapon.

"We in the National-Socialist High Command," he said, as he reverted to French and his demeanor moderated from menacing to merely pompous, "are acutely aware of the injustices inflicted on the Breton peoples by the archaic feudal covenant still enforced by the local seigneurs and condoned, nay, encouraged by the elitist central government."

He paused to gauge the effect his pontificating had on us, and he looked at Jakez as though expecting a response, which was clearly dangerous.

"Alas, mein Herr," I interjected, "we are fishermen, and although we work long, hard hours, we are mostly self-employed; so we do not live under the same rules as farm laborers."

"Well," he continued. "You will find that the German occupying forces, ably supported by your loyal Vichy government, will improve the lot of both the land workers and the fishermen of Brittany. Tell me, is your friend able to walk? If not, perhaps I can arrange a vehicle to bring him down to the quay."

"P-please," I stammered, alarmed for a moment he might be sincere, "don't trouble yourself. I'm sure we'll manage just fine." I paused, grasping for subterfuge. "I believe the doctor has a car," I added hastily.

"Very well," he said, pulling a notebook and pen from his pocket and scribbling something down. "Here, take this; this will serve as a safe-conduct through the town. That is my name at the top. Don't hesitate to try to find me if you encounter difficulties."

"Thank you, Herr Major," I said, incredulously, as I stared down at this unanticipated bounty.

Jakez, who apparently realized that the scales were tipping slightly in our direction, nudged me in the ribs.

"Ask him about the *Kenavo*," he said, ever the practical seaman.

"And our fishing boat, Herr Major?" I asked. "My captain wishes to know if we can leave it here safely while we pick up our shipmate."

"*Bien sûr!*" he replied, taking back our precious pass and adjoining a hasty postscript. He handed it back with a flourish. "This gives you three days, my Breton compatriot. That should be more than enough time."

With that, he clicked his heels, threw his right arm in the air and rendered the obligatory: "*Heil Hitler!*" Then the two men clambered back onto their machine and disappeared back between the same two buildings.

Jakez shook his head in disbelief. "Did he say what I thought he said?"

"He did," I affirmed. "According to him, the only reason the Nazis came to Brittany is to help Breton peasants overthrow their bourgeois French oppressors. But whatever—as long as we have this pass, we can come and go as we please."

Jakez nodded, then stepped forward with a satisfied smirk and spat on the ground where the Major stood just moments before.

We battened down and lashed a tarpaulin over the *Kenavo* and ventured into the town. This once proud capital of Brittany had been in German hands for just two weeks, and disbelief and even shame were palpable on the faces of the people as they hurried through the streets with heads down and eyes averted.

We found our doctor's house—a three-story Victorian with roof turret and brick façade—just as the shadows of early evening began stretching into twilight.

When we tapped lightly on the heavy oak door, a woman's voice, more suspicious than nervous, called from within: "Who are you and what do you want?"

"We are Breton fishermen, and we're here in search of a ship-mate. We were told that Dr. Bertrand might be able to help us."

"Just a minute," came the response, and we heard footsteps, retreating—fading.

Moments later, heavier, slower steps returned, and then a man's voice called out from behind the door: "This friend of yours, does he have a name?"

The moment I responded, the door cracked open and a balding middle-aged man with a heavy moustache peered out into the gloom.

"What makes you think your friend is here?" he asked, as his eyes darted nervously up and down the street.

"We were given this address by one of his army comrades," I explained. "This is his father, and I am Padrig Le Bras, an old shipmate and friend. We are here to bring him home. Your patient will vouch for us."

With that the doctor relaxed, and he opened the door wider and stepped aside. "Come in quickly, both of you. The curfew goes into effect soon, and they arrest people who venture on the street at night."

He ushered us into his surgical waiting room. "Please, gentlemen, sit. It must have been a difficult journey." He turned then to Jakez. "Did you come by train, Monsieur Le Corr?"

"Monsieur Le Corr speaks very little French," I interjected. "Do you speak Breton?"

The doctor shook his head apologetically. "No, I'm afraid not. But this is unfortunate; I have bad news, and I would rather disclose it personally."

My heart sank. "Oh God, no, he can't be dead, can he?"

"Your friend has been through hell these last few weeks," he replied. "But, no. He's not dead. But—and I'm very sorry to have to tell you this—last week we had to amputate his left leg at the knee. It couldn't be avoided; gangrene was setting in."

I glanced at my companion, but he had not followed the conversation. But when I translated the appalling news, his head slowly sank into his hands and he turned away in despair.

Dr. Bertrand continued: "Your friend is hidden upstairs under the mansard. Come, I will show you the way."

I tried to put my arm around Jakez's shoulders, but he shook it off roughly and we followed the doctor up the main stairs to a landing overlooking the foyer.

The doctor pointed to a huge ornamental washstand that stood against the wall. "If you lift that to one side," he said, "you will find a detachable panel which conceals a stairway to the attic. They will take you to your son." He pulled a watch from his vest pocket and snapped open the top. "You may go up and see him now. But be careful. He will probably be asleep, and he sleeps with a service revolver under his pillow. If you startle him, he may shoot."

As soon as we removed the panel, Jakez called up to his son in Breton and followed his voice up the stairs.

The doctor and I lingered on the landing to give them a few moments alone. There was a short, uncomfortable silence, and then we both began speaking simultaneously.

The doctor held up his hands: "I'm sorry," he said. "What were you going to say?"

"Do you think he is fit to travel?" I repeated.

"That's a difficult question to answer," he replied. "In a perfect world, of course, I'd have to say no—especially not on a fishing boat. But under these dire circumstances, I don't think we have much of a choice. There will never be a better opportunity to return him to his home and family."

I agreed with that assessment—we had a pass to get us through the town; the boat was ready to sail, and I knew that Jakez would never leave without his son. So we began discussing any other difficulties we might encounter.

And while we stood there on the landing, a tall woman, her iron-gray hair swept back into a chignon, ascended the stairs with a tray of bandages.

She and the doctor exchanged smiles and he placed his arm around her shoulders when she joined us. "This is Nicole—my wife, my nurse and my right hand. She has been taking care of your friend, and I see it's time to change his dressings."

We exchanged greetings, and then she slipped into the narrow stair well. The good doctor waved me in behind her, and the winding stairs brought me to a box room tucked directly beneath the slate and lath of the roof.

I admit I had not known what to expect when I stepped into the room, but when I saw the figure lying on the floor in that cramped and dusty space, I scarcely recognized him.

Gone was the sturdy, self-reliant young man I had sailed beside for more than a dozen years; in his place was a defeated soldier with haggard features and sunken eyes. These features were accentuated by the shadows thrown from an oil lamp on the floor beside the mattress. I knelt beside Yann and took his hand, and was rewarded by a wan smile:

"Padrig, Padrig," he said weakly, "I feared I would never see you again."

I glanced up at his father as I struggled to find words. In his devastation, Jakez had also been unable to comfort his son sufficiently.

I turned back to the boy, put my arms around him and kissed his cheeks. But in the end, all I could manage was a weak, "thank God you're alive," and I lowered my eyes in shame.

Mercifully, the doctor's wife set her tray down beside me and began preparations for changing Yann's bandages.

I pulled myself to my feet, took his father by the arm and pulled him gently to one side. "At least we have him back," I whispered.

He nodded grimly, but there was no joy in those eyes.

During the next few days, I came to realize that my old friend was having great difficulty coming to terms with two inescapable facts: the sudden collapse of the invincible French army, after his comrades and he had struggled for four years in the trenches of the Great War; and the loss of his boy as a shipmate and fellow fisherman.

In the Brittany of the thirties and forties, to lose one's only son's wage-earning capacities was a calamity, but to have to nurse and financially support an amputee, in addition, was a devastating burden.

On the third day, we loaded Yann into the doctor's Citroën CV and brought him down to the river where the *Kenavo* chafed at her moorings, eager to carry him home. And because his patient was still weak from his surgery, the good doctor helped us bring him on board and make him comfortable on a field cot of fishing nets. Dr. Bertrand then cast off our lines and wished us God speed as we fired up our motor and pushed out into the Loire to begin our return voyage.

As we island-hopped our way back up the coast, our passenger spent most of the first day in a drug-induced sleep. But by the second afternoon the salt air and the gentle roll of the ocean seemed to be having a healthful effect, so he sat in the stern and I made him comfortable by propping up his stump with my duffel bag and offered him the helm.

"Here," I said, with a wink. "If you can't pay for your passage, you are going to have to work for it."

His contented expression told me all I needed to know as he grasped the tiller and ran a practiced eye over the trim of the sail. Then he looked out to the south-west over the vast expanse of the Atlantic Ocean and filled his lungs with air laced with the salt and spray of a thousand waves.

"This is where the Good Lord would want me to spend my days, Padrig," he said. "And that's exactly what I intend to do from this moment on."

It was good to see Yann in such a positive frame of mind after all he'd been through, and we bantered back and forth, just as we had when he was a boy. And when he asked how we came to find him, I entertained him with a lighthearted version of our preparations and our outbound voyage, making sure to emphasize his father's critical role.

"But you," I said, when I had finished. "How did you end up in Nantes, of all places?"

"That's a long story," he replied. "And I don't have anything like your story-telling skills. But if you'll bear with me, I'll do my best."

13

Yann Le Corr

The regiment is stationed along the Maginot Line—on the edge of the Ardennes—two leagues from the Belgian border, and we are bivouacked under canvas. High Command puts us to work digging trenches: all day we are digging trenches, a maze of stupid trenches. In the evenings we sit around in our tents playing cards, drinking cheap wine and telling tales from home—tales of our farmsteads, our boats, our families. These stories help to bring us together and remind us why we are here and what we are fighting for.

When our captains decide the trenches are ready, they call down the bigwigs, who come to inspect them. There are meetings at Battalion headquarters with parades and inspections—all the usual bullshit. First they make us dig through a mountain of mud, and then they expect us to get all cleaned up for a fucking parade. I tell you, Padrig, the military has some really stupid plans for winning this war. Just because they won the last one, they think this one's going to be a snap.

But they don't like our trenches or our position. They think we are too exposed. So they pull us back to the next hill and we start over. Twice they pull this shit—it's like they want us to dig trenches all the way back to Paris. But for me, the worst part is not the digging: it's the enemy spy planes. Every day they fly overhead—watching us: it's noisy and creepy. But does anyone try to shoot them down or chase them off? Nah! That would be too easy.

Then it begins! No more spy planes. Now the air is filled with Stukas raking our lines and positions with machine-gun fire. Then their artillery starts, and the sky is black with shells and mortars. The bombardment lasts for two days—we just sit in our trenches with our heads down. On the second day regimental headquarters takes a direct hit, killing our colonel and his second-in-command.

When we hear this, my sergeant tells me that is the end of our regiment as a fighting machine. He says they were only officers we had who knew what they were doing. According to him the rest of the staff officers got their commissions from political pandering—whatever that means. And our field officers, he says, are a joke—just kids—wet behind the ears.

On the third day comes the big push—wave upon wave of tanks, with infantry battalions moving in behind. We try to hold 'em off, but it's like trying to hold back the tide—men are dying all around me. But it's the noise that gets to me. The crash of guns; the screams of the wounded—it was Hell.

The sergeant receives word from field HQ: "Begin withdrawing your men in an orderly fashion!"

Who do they think they're kidding? There's nothing orderly about being in Hell. Some men throw down their rifles and start running. When I see that, I want to run, too—I'm just as scared as they are—but I'm in the same trench as the sergeant. But when he climbs out of the hole to stop the stampede, he's cut to pieces by machine-gun fire and his body falls back into the trench right on top of me.

That's enough for me! I'm getting the fuck out. We're all getting out. I heave his body to one side, scramble out of the fox hole and start running. I tell you, Padrig, I never ran so far or so fast in my life. But when the cannon roar fades and the killing is far behind me, I collapse on the outskirts of a forest settlement and lie on the ground gasping for air.

When my body stops heaving and I climb to my feet, I realize to my shame that my face and coat are covered with my sergeant's blood. I finally pull myself together and team up with another soldier from my regiment who comes running in behind me, and together we head into the village, slinking between the homes like a couple of thieves. And then another Breton *poilu* calls to us from a house on the square. Now there are three of us in this bombed-out settlement not knowing what to do or where to go.

Then the artillery bombardment starts again and the soldier in the doorway leads us inside and down to the cellar. And behind the cellar's dense rock walls, I feel safe for the first time in days and begin to relax. But we're all frightened and exhausted, so we agree to stay there and rest up until dark and then try to make our way back to our lines—wherever the fuck they might be.

Here we sit, three Breton peasant soldiers in the cellar of a house in an abandoned village. Shells are flying overhead, and we have no idea where the Germans are, where the French are, or where we are. I am sitting on the floor with my back against a stone wall. Sitting beside me is Gael Le Bris, a farm laborer from the Black Mountains, and across from us is Marcel Guillou, a miller's son from Malestroit, on the Lanvaux Heath, north-east of Vannes.

Marcel though is the first among us to shake off his funk, and he is soon restless, getting to his feet and poking around, testing the doors and peering into the cabinets. "Aha!" he says, as he holds up a key, ignoring the inferno outside. "This is more like it." He returns to the only locked door, unlocks it and swings it open and disappears inside.

Gael turns a frightened face toward me. "What?" he says.

"Beats the hell out of me," I say, shaking my head. But our eyes are on the doorway. Where has he gone? What is he doing?

Marcel reappears with three bottles under his arm. "This'll make the day go better," he says.

We are suddenly very thirsty, and we jump to our feet.

"Is it cider?" asks Gael, doubtfully.

"No. They don't make cider around here," says Marcel. "It's wine, red wine!"

He passes out the bottles, and I seize mine and pick at the cork with my bayonet. It refuses to budge. I jab at it but only succeed in stabbing my fingers. Frustrated, I shove the damn thing down into the bottle.

At last the wine is mine—my only victory in this crazy war. I hold my captive up by its neck. "May Hitler rot in Hell," I say. "*Ar Breizh!*"

I'm not saluting my home because I'm patriotic; I am railing at a God that so easily allows all this war and shit happen to us. What the hell did we do?

"*Ar Breizh,*" they echo, and we take long pulls at our bottles, none of us knowing whether we will ever see our homeland again.

The wine is rich and dry. It rolls down my throat and through my body, warming me as it passes, numbing my senses. The hell outside begins to fade as I wipe my mouth with the back of my hand and stumble against the wall. Marcel is standing in the middle of the room, savoring a mouthful. But it is Gael, shell-shocked and frightened Gael, who captures the moment. He is sitting back on the floor leaning against the wall and gazing reverently at his bottle:

"Jesus!" says he. "That'll settle your fucking nerves."

We say no more until our bottles are empty. By this time I am back on the floor next to Gael, and we are both watching Marcel, who is rocking gently back and forth with his eyes closed. Then another shell lands, just missing the house, but the impact throws him to the ground. He picks himself back up, curses the air, and hurls his flagon at the wall.

"Those Nazi pigs," he says indignantly. "Don't they know it's the cocktail hour?" He dusts himself off. "Let's get some more bottles." he says, as an impish grin lights up his filthy, war-torn face.

This seems like a good idea to me, but Gael is not so sure. "I don't know, Marcel," he cautions. "We don't want to get drunk."

"Why the hell not?" says Marcel. "We could be dead at any moment. Let's go out with a bang. Tell him, Yann."

"Just one more bottle, Gael," I say. "It will keep our spirits up while we wait for dark. Don't worry, my friend. We won't leave you down here."

Marcel chuckles at that as he dives back into the stock and returns with three more bottles. "Here," he says, affecting a French accent. "Try a thirty-eight; one of my better years."

There's no mercy for the cork this time when I grasp my bayonet, and I drive it straight down into the bottle and take a long pull at the wine. Meanwhile Marcel has pitched one to Gael, but it slips between his fingers and drops to the floor, exploding at his feet.

"Damn!" he says. And he stares down at the puddle of wine as though it were his own blood.

"After all the crap we've been through today, that's nothing— nothing!" says Marcel. "There's plenty more where that came from. Here, catch this." He tosses over the other bottle and dives back into the stock room. Soon bottles come rolling out along the floor.

"Help yourselves, boys," his voice calls from deep within the cellar, just before another shell hits the house next to ours.

I don't remember how long we are down there—I guess I fall asleep. But the next thing I know, a boot is kicking me in the ribs.

"*Raus, raus!*" I hear. I open my eyes and find myself staring straight up at a rifle barrel. "On your feet! *Hände hoch! Raus, raus!*" Teutonic roars fill the room.

I look around me. Marcel is on his feet with his hands in the air, and Gael is picking himself off his knees.

They take us outside and herd us with other prisoners in the village square. And there we stand with our hands on our heads while they search the rest of the buildings. Then they lock us in the village hall for the night. And as darkness falls on our makeshift prison the cannons of Hell go strangely silent.

There are about twenty prisoners in the hall, but only five of us are from Brittany. We group together in the back of the room. And as usual, Marcel is nosing around behind a platform.

When he comes back, he has news: "There's a way out of here," he says. "And the forest is just beyond the building."

Gael and I are ready to follow him anywhere. If he can pull wine out of the air, he can get us out of this. "Fine," I say. "Anything's better than a German prison camp."

"What about them?" says Gael, jerking his thumb toward the other men standing around in small groups, talking quietly.

"To hell with them," says Marcel. "Besides, we don't speak French. How are we to let them know without telling the whole world?"

"I don't know. We can't just vanish." I am torn. Leaving them behind doesn't seem right. But I know we would have more chance of success on our own. "I can speak a few words," I offer. "There's an officer over there. Why don't I talk to him?"

I go to the officer, a captain of artillery, and ask him if he wants to try to escape, although I don't tell him how. But he's afraid the Germans will shoot him if someone tries it. I shrug and go back to the Breton group.

"He has cold feet," I say. "We're on our own."

"Okay," says Marcel. "Let's wait till everyone's asleep."

We all get down on the floor and pretend to settle in for the night. I actually do try to sleep, but my nerves are jangled from all the fighting, the running and the wine.

Finally, Marcel whispers in my ear: "Okay," he says. "It's time to go."

One by one, we five Bretons sneak under the platform and climb up and out through a coal chute. We find ourselves in a small enclosure at the back of the hall. There are no guards to be seen, and there are no lights except for a little moonlight. We wait for a few seconds, but no sound comes from the inside, so Marcel waves us on and leads us single file down a long alleyway to the edge of the forest.

We walk all night hoping we are going in the right direction. Finally, at daybreak we come to a river bank, and we follow it away from the morning sun, towards the west. Eventually we come to a bridge guarded by a German patrol.

"Now what?" growls Gael, who has found his fighting spirit again.

"Let's go back around the river bend and swim across," I offer.

But I'm the only man who can swim, so it's the bridge or nothing. And Marcel, who has become our leader, decides to take a closer look, and he motions to me to follow him.

"You men wait here," he says.

We creep up close to the road and onto a wooded knoll that gives us a clear view of the bridge. There are two guards at each end, and on our side there's a light truck parked alongside the road.

Marcel studies the scene for a moment, and then his eyes widen. "Okay," he says. "The key here is to get down to that truck without being noticed. Stay here and keep an eye on them. I'm going to get the others."

I take a closer look at the truck and see what got him excited: There are rifles stacked in the back.

I nod and turn back to the bridge while Marcel crawls back the way we came. While I am watching, one of the guards at our end sees something in the river and calls his companion over. Soon they are both leaning over the rail, completely distracted.

I know there will never be a better time to make our move, but Marcel and the others are nowhere to be seen. I don't know what comes over me, Padrig. I never before have the urge to be a hero.

But before I know it, I am creeping down the knoll to the back of the truck. I pull out a rifle. So far, so good. But from where I stand I can no longer see the guards. I glance back at the knoll and see Marcel and Gael peering down and motioning to me to stay still.

Suddenly Marcel jumps out and shouts: "Go, go!" And my four companions start running down from the knoll screaming their heads off.

I spin out from behind the truck, drop to one knee and lift the rifle to my shoulder. I shoot one guard in the chest as he turns toward me, but the other one runs across the road and puts the truck between us.

I jump to my feet as I feed another shell into the chamber. I run around the truck and suddenly we're face to face. We both have our rifles at the ready. It's now or never! I fire at him, point-blank. I feel a sledgehammer blow to my leg, and I buckle over and pitch forward onto the road.

I don't know how long I lay there, but I hear shouts and gunfire from the other end of the bridge, and the sound of a motor turning over. Then I hear Marcel's voice and I feel myself being lifted into the truck. Soon we are racing over the bridge with Gael and Marcel blazing away like a couple of gangsters. We make it across, I remember, but after that things get hazy. Marcel tells me later I pass out from the pain.

I know I spend a lot of time lying in the back of the truck, and I vaguely remember being told we're in the Loire Valley. Then I am moved to a French truck and the following day to a car. The next thing I know we're riding through the streets of Nantes. Gael and Marcel are still with me.

They tell me the rest: "When we get down to the truck," says Marcel, "we grab the two remaining rifles from the back and run to back you up. But we arrive just in time to watch you shoot it out with the German guards. You kill them both—great job. Meanwhile one of the other men cranks up the truck, and we put you in the back and head over the bridge as fast as we can go."

Gael picks up the story: "Then we hook up with a French convoy that is heading for the Loire Valley to make a stand. The other two men are placed in infantry units, but they send us back with you to seek medical aid. Eventually we meet up with Dr. Bertrand, who brings us back to his surgery in Nantes."

We hear on the radio that Pétain has sued for an armistice, and Marcel decides to head home before the Germans move in. He and Gael promise to find my father when they get back. And I guess you know the rest.

* * * *

Padrig Le Bras

When Yann finished his narrative, he searched his father's eyes for a reaction—encouragement, perhaps, or sympathy—but if he expected any, he was surely disappointed. Jakez simply grunted as he got to his feet to adjust the sail.

But then he turned to me, and I was looking into the eyes of a young man—a boy, really—who had seen so much in so short a time. He had been a player on the world's stage for just a millisecond and had paid dearly for that privilege. What could I say to him? What words were there to comfort him? For the remainder of his time on this earth he would struggle just to walk. Perhaps he could still fish for a living, but it wouldn't be easy.

Yann was born into a world of poverty, where his only assets were his healthy body and youthful vigor. And now they had been ripped from him because of one impetuous moment of solidarity and patriotism. Even as I silently raged against the cruel implacability of fate, I reached over and placed a supporting arm around his shoulder. But even I, Padrig the Raconteur, had no words of comfort for my friend. For I knew only too well there was no solace I could offer that would have even a grain of validity. We sat there together in the stern forlornly clutching each other as ocean swells gently rocked our tiny vessel.

The following afternoon, we dropped anchor in Kérity harbor.

14

When I returned to my farmstead, I found everything in order. It was as though I had left for an hour, not a fortnight. Jacqueline had apparently taken everything in her stride. Indeed, as I entered she was happily sketching at the kitchen table. It was as though she had lived there for years.

"Are you sure you weren't born a peasant?" I said, as I folded her into my arms.

"I have momentous news," she said, when we finally separated. "But first I have to hear a full accounting of your adventures. Start from the moment we picked up the fishing permits and omit nothing. I'll make coffee."

An hour later, Jacqueline was torn between her joy on the success of our mission and her sadness at Yann's terrible wounds. Indeed, this upset her so much that I had to remind her she had news of her own to convey.

"Oh, yes, my news," she said. "It pales by comparison to your story, I must say, but it's still quite important. At least it is to me. Jean-Pierre is back from the front, too. He marched onto the farm two days ago accompanied by a child. Did you know he had a son?"

"That is good news," I said. "And I do remember something about a boy. He's eight or nine, yes?"

"He's nine. He said his ex-wife begged him to bring the boy back here with him. Paris is dangerous. Nazis are rounding up Jews and shipping them off to labor camps."

"But what is he going to do with him in Brittany?"

"He wants to move back in to Alain's cottage and simply lay low for the duration."

"But his ex-wife? If the boy was in danger she must be, too."

"She's going to stay in Paris and look after her parents. Apparently, they're very unworldly and do not believe they are in any danger." Jacqueline screwed up her face in disgust. "I quite understand that they would think like that. Such barbarity is very difficult to believe. It's the twentieth century, for God's sake!"

I nodded sympathetically, although to my mind the archaic, almost feudal, landholding system in Brittany and the way landowners treated the local peasants, made what the Nazis conquerors were doing very easy to believe. And the fact that it was the twentieth century simply made my despair for the human race more acute.

I sat down across from her at the table and changed the subject: "Are you going to move back in with Jean-Pierre?"

She shook her head regretfully. "I don't think so," she said. "Now he has the boy, there's a religious complication. Jean-Pierre promised his wife he wouldn't do anything immoral under the same roof as his son. But even if that weren't the case, there would still be an obstacle: Ephraim, that's the boy's name, is an *enfant terrible*."

Jacqueline grimaced as she spoke those words, then continued. "He hates the cottage; he hates the countryside. He thinks Alain's farm and the animals in the barnyard stink to high heaven. He never stops complaining. I've never heard anything like it. You're my friend, Padrig, so I can be frank with you. I can't stand the little monster."

"Come now, Jacqueline," I said, as I took a sip from a fresh cup of coffee. "He can't be that bad."

"Oh, no?" she replied. "When I go over there he won't even speak to me. He doesn't include me in their conversation. He speaks to his father in Yiddish. Jean-Pierre explained that he's attached to his mother and can't understand why he had to leave her. But if you ask me, he's just a rude little brat. And if Jean-Pierre doesn't do something about his attitude shortly, they're not going to be safe whatever they do or wherever they go."

"But what about you?" I asked. "What are you going to do? Are you going back to your mill studio?"

"No, I can't do that either. My landlord has filled it with refugees from the east. I wouldn't be comfortable there anymore—there's no room for my work. I don't know what I'm going to do. I can't go home. My parents live in Soissons, just north of Paris. I honestly think I'd be safer here."

"Then why don't you stay with me?" I said. "There's plenty to do. With you watching the farm, I can spend more time fishing. Jakez's going to need help now that he has his son to take care of."

"I'd like that very much; thank you. I was hoping you would ask. But what are we going to do about Ephraim? Just because I don't like him doesn't mean I want him taken away by the Nazis."

I didn't know what to tell her. I had no experience in dealing with pampered children. Breton peasants work from dawn to dusk just to put food upon the table, and children are expected to pull their weight from the time they are able to walk and talk.

"Let's walk over there and say hello," I said. "I need to talk to Jean-Pierre about what he's going to do now. This way I can meet this problem child and determine if he is as bad as you say."

After we finished our coffee, we walked the half league that separated our two homes. And as we drew near, Jean-Pierre came running out onto the porch, his face beaming with delight.

"Padrig!" he cried, as he embraced me enthusiastically. "It's so good to see you, my friend. Come into the house. Come meet Ephraim."

I was moved by his affirmation of our friendship.

"So, Padrig," he continued, when he eventually stepped back. "Where have you been? What have you been doing? Jacqueline wouldn't tell me anything; she said it was a secret—part of the war effort. Does this mean you have become a follower of de Gaulle? What did he call it?" He paused and scratched his head. "Oh yeah," he continued, with a smile. "Have you joined *La Résistance*?"

"No," I said, shaking my head. "I don't think there is any organized resistance as of yet. But I'm sure that will change. No, I went with Jakez to bring his son back from the war. Did you hear what happened to him?"

Jean-Pierre nodded: "It's terrible, terrible! Poor Yann, what's he going to do now? How's he going to survive?"

As we were speaking we entered the cottage, and I saw the boy sitting in the corner; his sullen expression plain to see. His father spoke to him, introducing me. But Ephraim didn't answer, and his eyes didn't move. Then, after a long, uncomfortable silence, he turned to his father and mumbled a few words in a language I took to be Yiddish.

I also turned to Jean-Pierre: "Doesn't he speak French?" I asked.

"Oh, yes. He was born in Paris. But he's confused. His mother kept him secluded from the world. He spent the last year at a yeshiva reading Hebrew texts and studying the Talmud. She wants him to be a rabbi like his grandfather."

"Well," I said. "You'd better make it very clear that here in Brittany, and especially during the Nazi occupation, there's going to be no room for stubborn little boys. He will do as he's told or soldiers will come and take him away. This is not a game!"

"I've been trying to tell him that. Maybe you'll have better luck getting through to him."

"You know, Jean-Pierre, in Nantes they are already searching for Jews and rounding them up. Are you sure you're going to be safe here?"

He shrugged. "I'm going to do what I was doing before: work with you; work with Alain; work with Jakez. Who's going to stop me? And you said it yourself—I can disappear into the woodwork."

"You fit right in before the war," I said. "But there aren't many Bretons with children who speak Yiddish and study Hebrew. What are you going to do about Ephraim?"

By this time the boy was sitting up and taking notice. Apparently, he had only just realized he was in danger.

"But, why, why?" he cried, plaintively. "What have we done to these Germans?"

As he was now speaking French, I assumed he had deigned to include me in his conversation, and I decided to take advantage of that while I had the chance.

I went over and grasped him by the shoulders. "Listen, Ephraim," I said. "It doesn't really matter that you haven't done anything. All we know is that the Nazis are rounding up all the Jews they can find and putting them in detention centers. And if you don't want to go with them, you'd better do exactly as we say. Do you understand me?"

His face lost a little of that sullen expression as my words began to sink in. "What do you want me to do?" he whined.

15

From that moment on, we managed to bring a little normalcy back to our surroundings. We were far removed from any large town, so we weren't bothered much by the occupying troops. The nearest garrison of any size was several leagues away at Pont l'Abbé. For identification purposes, Jacqueline became my niece and Jean-Pierre became a peasant named Jean-Pierre Le Fer. However, there was no simple identity that would fit his son. The local elementary school taught only in Breton. So we decided he would have to disappear. Ephraim Goldfeldt would no longer officially exist.

Jean-Pierre slipped easily back into his old routine, working on Alain's farm or my farm and fishing on the *Kenavo*. In the evenings both he and his son took lessons in Breton with Jacqueline. Jean-Pierre soon became proficient enough to fool the Germans, which was all he really needed. As for Ephraim, once he began to speak a few words of Breton, he began playing with Alain's brood of children, which meant that he, at long last, was also beginning to melt into the landscape. Or so it seemed to us at the time.

Meanwhile, Jacqueline, Jean-Pierre and I gathered most evenings around the radio to listen to Radio Free France, which was broadcast from London every evening at seven o'clock. Then we would listen to Radio Vichy and hear Pétain's slant on things. We guessed the truth was somewhere between the two, although it was easier to believe de Gaulle. Even when the British Navy destroyed the French fleet near Oran, killing 1,300 French sailors, de Gaulle managed to explain it away, saying that Naval Command had refused to rally around the Allied flag, and thus, regrettably, the Allies had to prevent the fleet from falling into enemy hands.

Jacqueline continued to work on *Fishermen of Kérity* in my farmhouse, and it was taking shape rather well. I never tired of looking at it. But when she wasn't working on the painting, she complained incessantly that we weren't doing enough, or indeed, anything at all to rid ourselves of the Nazi pigs, as she called the occupying forces.

"You must be more patient." I said, time and time again. "Opportunities will arise. We must wait for them and learn to recognize it when they show themselves."

* * * *

Because our farms were off the beaten track and adjoining some largely uncultivated, wooded heath land, Alain and I only came into direct contact with the Nazi authorities once a week. Each Friday one of their trucks would appear to take away our tithe—that percentage of our produce taken to sustain the occupying army. Fortunately, we both had barns upon the heath where we could store and conceal a percentage of our crops.

And in order to coordinate our evasions, it became the norm to meet on Thursday evenings to prepare our stories. It was during these informal get-togethers that I first learned that all was not well on my neighbor's farm. Jean-Pierre paid Alain's wife to watch his son when he was fishing, but according to her, the boy was a liar, and worse than that—he was a thief.

"In fact," she continued after she brought up the subject, "he takes everything and anything that isn't nailed down—and sometimes even that's not safe. You'd better be careful, Padrig. Ephraim's been straying farther and farther afield. You'd better watch your property."

I didn't pay much attention to Jeanne-Marie, because I knew she tended to exaggerate, and there were much too many other things to worry about. But one day when Jean-Pierre and I sailed into Kérity harbor on the *Kenavo*, I was surprised to see Ephraim standing on the dock, surrounded by local urchins.

"Isn't that your son?" I asked, pointing to the knot of boys on the quay.

"Yes," said Jean-Pierre. "I managed to find him a bicycle. He gets so bored staying on the farm."

"But isn't that dangerous? What about the Germans?"

"They've got quite enough to worry about, without going around questioning little boys. Besides, Ephraim's Breton is much better these days. I only wish mine were half as good."

When we were riding home later that day, Jean-Pierre asked me about the fishing schedule.

"Who sets up the boat crews, Padrig? Is it you, or is it Jakez? If it's you, I'll tell you now; I'd like a break from working with Jakez. Now that I understand Breton, he spends most of our time on the water complaining."

I knew exactly what he meant. I had been getting the same treatment. Jakez also had to share his catch with the Nazis, and his was all but impossible to hide—a full fifty per cent would be siphoned off each and every time he landed his boat. His tirades on the subject were endless, sometimes lasting the entire time we were out on the water.

"The last time I was out with him," Jean-Pierre continued, "he was on a rampage. He spared no one: the French Army; the Vichy Government; de Gaulle; he even began harping on about Jews."

"What have Jews done to Jakez?" I laughed.

"Oh, he was rambling on about an international Jewish banking conspiracy, something about how Jewish bankers bled Germany dry during the Twenties, thereby directly causing massive inflation and the war. It was scary listening to him. Where would a fisherman who speaks only Breton come up with an idea like that?"

"He must have been listening to radio propaganda," I replied. "He understands some French. What else could it be?"

"I don't know. But I'll tell you, Padrig, I'm getting sick of it."

* * * *

The following week, Jacqueline and I were at work in the barnyard; she was feeding the livestock, and I was cleaning out the pigsties. It was a warm, sunny morning, and when we stopped at noon for our lunch, we brought it out onto the back porch. It was our usual fare—hearth-smoked pork sausage, Jeanne-Marie's home-baked bread, cheese and cider.

The advantage with having one's own farmstead during these dark times was that for us there was very little food shortage. And since the Nazis had forbidden the sale of alcohol to anyone except themselves, it was nice to have a cider press.

So there we were sitting in the sun enjoying our little respite—at least, I certainly was, when Jacqueline once again brought up the subject of resistance.

"There must be something we can do," she said.

"I'm sure you're right," I replied, wearily. "But I don't know what that something is. From the stories I hear, Bretons are being arrested every day for tiny, meaningless acts of defiance. They annoy the German High Command by doing or saying something stupid and get themselves thrown in jail. Now, you tell me, what did they prove? What did they gain?"

As I turned toward her, I noticed an unusual movement in the bushes behind Jacqueline's shoulders on the other side of the barnyard. And because there was no wind, there was no immediate explanation.

She noticed my eyes narrow and began to turn her head to follow my gaze; but I reached out and touched her hand.

"Don't make any sudden movements," I said quietly. "There's something out there in the bushes at the bottom of the hill, but I'm not quite sure what it might be—a deer perhaps, or even a wild boar."

"So what if it is!" she muttered, still angry from our previous discussion. "Didn't you have to turn in your hunting rifle to the Germans? What do you think you're going to do—hit it over the head with a bucket of slops?"

I smiled at that. "Yes, I gave them my rifle, but I still have a shotgun."

That brought a faint sneer to Jacqueline's face: "Was that your own personal tiny, but meaningless, act of defiance?" she snorted, as she turned and peered into the undergrowth. "I don't see anything. Whatever was there must have gone by now."

"Maybe, but maybe not; I'll get my gun, and we'll go take a look."

I loaded my shotgun, wrapped it in an old potato sack, and we walked over to the bottom of the hill. But after nosing around the bushes for a while, I pointed to the cart track leading up to the heath: "Why don't you look up there? I'm going to poke around down here awhile longer and see if I can find some tracks."

She nodded and began moving up the path, and I turned back toward the road. But as I eased myself between two spiny gorse bushes, the glint of metal caught my eye. It was a child's bicycle: the same one that Ephraim had been astride when I saw him on the wharf.

What was he doing on my farm? I recalled Jeanne-Marie's warning. Was he up to no good?

It didn't seem possible, but if he was here for a visit, he would have ridden right up to the farmhouse. But maybe he was hiking up on the heath. I decided to give him the benefit of the doubt and started up the cart track after Jacqueline.

When I was close to the top of the hill, I found Jacqueline sitting on the ground with her back against a tree trunk. "Come on, old timer!" she called. "The boar is probably on the other side of the heath by now."

I shook my head vigorously as I walked up to her. And as I reached down to pull her to her feet, I explained what I found.

"What does that mean, I wonder?" she asked.

"Oh, he's probably exploring up here on the heath somewhere."

"What do you think he's doing?"

"I don't know. Maybe he heard about the prehistoric rock formations up here; there's a cairn and a couple of stone dolmen on the property. Or perhaps he's hunting rabbits. There could be lots of reasons."

We were walking as we talked and reached the top of the hill, and from the cover of the trees, we could look across the heath. It was dappled with yellow gorse, deep purple heather and coarse grass, gaudy with bluebells, celandines and all the colors of the season. And on the other side of the clearing, under a large copper beech, was a barn that had been on the property as long as my family had been the tenant farmers.

"Since we've come this far," I said, "let's walk over there and check on the barn. You haven't seen it before, but that's part of the farmstead, too."

We went in opposite directions, each skirting the meadow from the cover of the woods until we met again by the building. However, there was no sign of the boy. But when I went around the back of the barn, I saw signs of an attempted break-in. There were scuffs on the wall and a crack in one of the wooden shutters where someone had tried to pry it open.

"Somebody has been here recently," I said, pointing to the shutter, "but whoever it was is long gone. We may as well head back."

I was reluctant to voice my suspicions, but we both knew who had tried to force the shutter. And when we drew closer to the farm, it was evident that we had yet another problem. There was a lot of squawking coming from the hen house.

"The little bastard is in there stealing your eggs!" said Jacqueline, as we ran across the yard toward the noise.

We reached the door just as it swung open to reveal Ephraim crouching inside with a wicker panier filled with eggs.

"Got you, you little shit!" she screamed, as I grabbed his arm and she pulled the basket out of his hands. "You're in for it now."

We took him into the farmhouse and sat him in the kitchen while we decided what to do with him.

"Was it you who tried to break into my building on the heath?" I asked him.

"I just wanted to see what was inside," he muttered, sullenly.

"Well," I said. "Let's get your bicycle and go take a look, shall we?"

I had had a sudden inspiration. Since he couldn't break into the barn, perhaps he couldn't break out of it, either. And if we let him cool his heels in there for a while, he might learn his lesson. It was at least worth trying.

* * * *

An hour later, I was back in the farmhouse, pulling off my clogs.

"How long are you going to leave him there?"

"I think two nights—that should be enough—two days and nights without food should make him realize that the world is not a playground for naughty little boys, and that it's time for him to listen to his elders. What do you think?"

"What about his father? He will go out of his mind with worry if we don't tell him."

"Jean-Pierre has been much too easy on the boy; Ephraim needs discipline, not coddling. The way it stands right now, he is a danger to us all. But, of course, if he comes here looking for him, I will tell him where I put him. But nonetheless, I will recommend that we leave him there until he learns to behave himself."

Jacqueline looked surprised. "I'm seeing something in you that I never saw before, Padrig. You're tougher than I knew." She shook her head and smiled. "Go out and sit on the porch and make yourself comfortable. I'll bring you a mug of cider."

With that we settled down for the rest of the day and spent the evening discussing the resistance, and how we could possibly get involved without getting ourselves shot. As usual, my approach was much more cautious than Jacqueline's. But as a concession to her, I did agree that she should take some of our contraband produce and donate it to the refugees who had been swarming into Brittany over the last few weeks.

16

Of course, both Jacqueline and I assumed that as soon as Jean-Pierre realized his son was missing, he would rush over to us for counsel and assistance. However, the following morning, when no distraught parent appeared at our doorstep, we returned to the heath fully expecting to find that our prisoner had escaped. Jacqueline carried up some food on the off chance we were wrong.

When I pulled back the door, however, he was still there, crouching in the sudden burst of daylight and squinting up at us defiantly. I wanted to wring his scrawny neck. Jacqueline gave him his food, which he promptly threw to the ground, and we locked him up once again.

On the way back to the farm, I repeated my objections. "We should have taken the food away, too. He wouldn't be so belligerent after starving for a few days."

But Jacqueline refused to argue the point; she simply slipped her arm in mine and smiled at me indulgently as we made our way down the narrow, overgrown track.

That day Jean-Pierre and I were slated to work the early-evening tide, and I left the farm at four in the afternoon to stop at his home and explain why I'd kidnapped his boy.

I rode through Alain's farm and up to the cottage in the back, distracted by a strange and eerie silence. And when I leaned my bicycle against the porch and walked to the door, it was not without a sense of foreboding.

There was no lock, and I knocked on the rough framework and pushed lightly against the door: "Jean-Pierre," I called. "Are you ready? Time and tide wait for no man."

But the scene within the cottage as the door swung open stopped me cold: Sitting at the table with a faint sneer upon his lips, and flanked by two Wehrmacht soldiers with drawn revolvers, was the same sergeant Jakez and I had encountered on the wharf the day we left for Nantes.

"So," he said, as he pulled himself casually to his feet. "We meet again, Mister, um—what did you say your name was, again?"

"I don't think the subject ever came up," I replied. "But you must have read it on my fishing permit: It's Padrig Le Bras."

"Ah, Padrig Le Bras, that's right. What's a fisherman like you doing so far away from the sea? And why are you sheltering a criminal?"

"Jean-Pierre sometimes works for me on my farmstead. We also fish together for some extra money."

"Did you know he is a Jew?"

"A what?" I asked, with a wooden expression.

"This man Jean-Pierre, who, according to you, works as a fisherman and a farm hand."

"His name is Jean-Pierre Le Fer. He is Breton," I said adamantly.

"Ahh, yes, Jean-Pierre Le Fer," repeated the sergeant, with a mocking lilt to his voice. "And just how long have you known this Monsieur Le Fer?"

Oh, no you don't, I thought. I may be a bumpkin, but I'm not going to fall for that one: "Since he moved back from Paris," I said, "in the summer of '39. Come to think of it, he must have lived there for a long time: he speaks French with a Parisian accent."

"How would you recognize someone speaking French with a Parisian accent?" he countered.

And as I prepared my reply, I mentally kicked myself for doing what I swore I wouldn't— volunteering more information than was absolutely necessary.

"In 1936 the French Socialist Government instituted paid vacations for factory workers, and people from all walks of life began to visit Brittany for the beaches. They stayed in local inns, and, because I am known for my storytelling abilities, I was sometimes engaged to entertain them in the evenings with local tales and legends. And, of course many of these people were from Paris."

The sergeant frowned as he digested this information. Then he nodded his head dismissively and moved on to the subject I'd been dreading: "What about his son? What can you tell me about him?"

I responded with another blank look: "I don't know about any son," I mumbled. "As far as I know he was never married."

"But, Monsieur Le Bras," the sergeant insisted, "we have found evidence of a boy living here."

"Perhaps one of Alain's children was staying here with him. I don't know; I live half a league up the road. I mind my own business."

The sergeant shook his head: "The boy staying here was studying Hebrew texts. That book over there on the dresser is the Talmud."

"It doesn't mean anything to me," I replied, truthfully, but I walked over and picked up the book anyway. I flipped through several pages, which were filled with strange characters, then shrugged my shoulders and snapped it shut.

"Tell me, Sergeant, what exactly is the problem here? Why have you arrested Jean-Pierre? What did he do, for Christ's sake?"

"He is a member of a subversive sub-human race who should not be mingling with normal people. And as such, he will be transported to Germany and placed in a labor camp."

"That has nothing to do with me," I protested. "May I go now? The tide is starting to recede, and I've got to get my nets out."

"You're going to jail. You're under arrest for conspiring to hide a fugitive."

"But…"

"First, you will take us to your farm, so we can search it for the missing Jew-boy. Then you will be taken to headquarters for further questioning."

The sergeant turned and barked out a command in German. One of the soldiers went outside and pulled a vehicle up to the cottage. And a few minutes later, I was back on my farm. The unexpected noise brought Jacqueline out onto the porch, and she stood there drying her hands on her apron as we approached.

"I've been arrested," I said to her, in Breton. "And so has Jean-Pierre. But I'm not sure exactly why, at this point."

"Does your wife speak French or German?" asked the sergeant.

"I speak French," responded Jacqueline, coldly. "Why have you arrested my uncle?"

"So, you are not Monsieur Le Bras' wife," replied the sergeant, with an ominous leer. "Is there a little boy here somewhere?"

"No, there isn't. But you don't have to take my word for it. Come see for yourself."

The sergeant barked more orders to his men and pointed to the outbuildings. He then told me to show them around.

"In the meantime," he smirked, "I will inspect the house and get acquainted with your charming niece."

Lots of luck, I thought, as I led the soldiers over to the pig sties. They didn't speak French, so I opened up each hut and gestured to them to peer inside. Then I took them over to the barn with the cider press and poured them both a mug of cider.

"May you rot in Hell," I said in Breton, as I passed them their drinks, thankful that Jacqueline couldn't hear me do the very thing I had been railing against since the invader marched into Brittany.

The soldiers drank two mugs of cider each, then we returned to the main house, and I studied the sergeant's face as they made their report. However, I wasn't able to read anything in his expression.

"So it seems that you have been telling us the truth," he said finally. "This makes me very happy, for I believed you were an honest man when I first met you. Now this has more or less confirmed it. And if you bring me a glass of whatever you have given to my men, I will forget I ever saw you at the Jew-boy's cottage."

I exchanged glances with Jacqueline; she looked upset. "What's the matter?" I asked, in Breton.

"That pig tried to fuck me," she replied. "He groped my body as though he owned it. It was disgusting."

"How did you get him to stop?"

"I bit his hand," she said, in the same matter-of-fact tone she would have used to report swatting a fly.

I glanced quickly at the sergeant and saw that one of his hands was wrapped in a towel, blood seeping through. He also looked very guilty, and I wondered just what the official Nazi policy was when it came to raping the women of a conquered people.

I also decided the best thing for me to do was to bring him some cider as quickly as possible to assuage this blow to his pride.

* * * *

After the soldiers left the farm, Jacqueline and I sat around the table, trying to make sense of what had happened.

"Somebody must have turned him in," she said. "There's no other reasonable explanation."

And although I couldn't for the life of me think who could have done such a thing, I agreed wholeheartedly. "But now we have to learn where they're keeping him," I added. "If we are going to help him at all, it has to be while he's in Brittany. Once they ship him east, he's lost."

"And what are we going to do about Ephraim? We can't just keep him locked in that barn on the heath."

"For now, that's exactly what we're going to do. While he's there he's safe, and he's going to stay there until I find out who betrayed them. I have to speak to Alain. He will probably know."

"Perhaps it was…. No. Forget it. It couldn't have been."

I looked at her sharply. "Who did you think it was? Alain's wife?"

She shook her head: "No," she said. "But I'm sure I am mistaken. I'm ashamed of my suspicions."

Jacqueline wouldn't tell me whom she had in mind, and we spent the rest of the evening speculating where they were keeping Jean-Pierre. Later, after she had gone to bed, I sat for a long time trying to make sense of it all—without much luck. Then I lay for most of the night inside my *gwele klos* staring into the darkness and wondering what was going to become of us all in this world gone mad.

* * * *

The next morning, I was sitting in my usual spot on the porch, sipping my coffee, when Jakez rode into view on his ancient bicycle. He leaned the bike against a post and dragged himself up the steps, his back bent. He looked very old.

"Do you want some coffee?"

He nodded, sat himself on a bench and began to roll a cigarette. And when I brought out his coffee he was staring out into space. I handed him the mug and he placed it beside him on the bench.

"What's on your mind?" I asked. "You never come out here this time of day."

"Where were you last night?" he replied. "We missed the evening tide. That's money down the drain, you know."

"I was arrested by the Nazis, and so was Jean-Pierre. They still have him locked up, but I don't know where."

"Serves him right," said Jakez. "That kid of his is a damned thief. He broke into my locker and stole some equipment."

The vehemence of his reply shocked me. "What did you do about it?" I asked, slowly, afraid I already knew the answer.

"I reported him to the harbor patrol, what else?"

"You mean… to the Germans?"

"What the hell would you do? That equipment cost money."

"Did you also tell them where he lives?" My voice was flat and very cold, and I was now on my feet.

Jakez looked at me and nodded his head slowly.

"Did you tell them he was a Jew, too?"

"I don't know. I may have."

"I don't believe it," I said. "Don't you know what that means?"

He lowered his eyes and nodded once again.

"Get off my property, Jakez! And don't come back. You're no longer welcome here."

He opened his mouth to say something else but thought better of it; he just put his coffee mug down on the bench and climbed slowly to his feet.

I watched him with a mixture of disgust and disbelief as he stumbled down the stairs and grasped his bicycle. He swung himself across the saddle and sat there for a moment, looking sadly in my direction. Then he pushed himself off and began to peddle toward the gate.

I heard a window open on the side of the house. *Oh, my God*, I thought, *Jacqueline!* I rushed inside. But it was too late.

I was just halfway across the kitchen when there was the blast of my shotgun. I stopped mid-stride as Jakez and his bicycle dropped to the ground, followed by a prolonged and deafening silence.

17

For a moment I was paralyzed. The unthinkable had happened. What should I do? Which way should I turn? Should I continue forward and rip the shotgun from Jacqueline's vengeance-seeking hands? Or turn back and do what I could for Jakez?

I felt helpless. My tiny world was spinning dangerously out of control. In the end I turned to the victim; I was too craven to confront the executioner.

Jakez lay face down, a meter or so beyond his bicycle, the back of his hemp-spun smock blood-red and ragged. The old fisherman would cast his nets no more. I knelt beside him but knew not why.

There was nothing I could do, and I stumbled to my feet as Jacqueline emerged from the building, shotgun at the ready; the glint in her eyes and the set of her jaw telling me that, if necessary, she was there to finish the job. Was this the same woman who had called me heartless the day before for withholding food from Ephraim?

"Is he dead?" Her voice was stony, distant.

"He is."

"It's no less than he deserved."

The sheer weight of these pitiless times pressed down upon my soul, and with shoulders bent and eyes lowered, I reached for the weapon, which she surrendered without protest.

* * * *

Later that morning I took my pickaxe and shovel to a clump of trees beyond the cider barn. There in a narrow clearing, with the thin Breton sunlight filtering through a canopy of oaks and beeches, I began to dig a grave. And as I swung the pickaxe over my head, Jakez's lifeless eye sockets stared reproachfully at me from the wheelbarrow where his body lay sprawled, awaiting interment.

Beneath my peasant's smock my chest heaved. I was burying a long-time friend and companion, someone with whom I had plucked the harvest of the wild Atlantic tides for some twenty years. But I knew deep in my soul, his betrayal of Jean-Pierre was indefensible, especially given his hatred of Germans. Jacqueline's justice had been, in my reluctant opinion, swift and meet.

She helped me lower Jakez into the pit, and then she stood across from me, her eyes avoiding mine, as I lowered in his bicycle and began shoveling the dark Breton soil over his blood-soaked corpse.

"What's our next move?" she asked; her voice barely more than a whisper.

Her question caught me by surprise, and I stopped for a moment and leaned upon my shovel.

"What do you mean?"

Her tear-moist eyes found mine for the first time that morning: "For God's sake, Padrig!" she cried, her voice rising. "The Nazis have Jean-Pierre; they're searching for Ephraim, and now—this?" She gestured toward the open pit.

"We know nothing about this," I said. "The Nazis arrested Jean-Pierre, they arrested me, and now Jakez has disappeared. Everyone will believe he was arrested, too."

"It's not the community I'm concerned about. What will the Nazis do—that Sergeant Weber, for example—when their collaborators disappear? They have to protect their sources of information or they will lose them."

"Jakez was not a collaborator," I responded angrily. "He fought valiantly for four long years against the Germans in the Great War. He was bitter and resentful—too upset to think straight." I threw another couple of shovelfuls into the pit, and the exertion helped to calm me. But when I looked back at Jacqueline, she was sobbing quietly. I stepped across the grave and put my arms around her.

"Don't cry," I said. "We have to stay strong. We have much to do. I wasn't accusing you or saying that you were wrong. If Jakez had come to me with his grievances I could have persuaded him to see reason, and he'd still be alive."

"And Jean-Pierre would still be free," she sobbed, defiantly.

I nodded.

"Padrig, what are we going to tell Yann?"

I shook my head. "Nothing," I said. "I'm too much of a coward. Besides, I don't think Yann would want to know his father was an informer. It's better this way."

I threw another shovelful of dirt into the pit and continued: "But as for Jean-Pierre, if we want to help him, we have to do it soon. Once they put him on a train, it will be too late. We don't even know where he is. We must locate him—and quickly."

"And the boy?"

Ephraim! What would we do—what *could* we do—with Ephraim? I tried to think of an answer, but none come. I stopped shoveling for a moment. I had lost my friend.

Jacqueline waited impatiently for a response, and I forced myself to turn my thoughts back to Ephraim. "I don't know," I said, "I don't know. This war has already wrecked so many lives. Do you have any thoughts?"

"Well," she said. "I think we should try to move him out of the region. But whatever we do we have to be very careful. If he gets caught now, we all go to jail—or worse. That German sergeant won't let you off the hook twice."

"When we have finished here," I said, "I will take Ephraim some food and tell him what happened to his father. The shock might bring him to his senses. After that, we might be able to work something out."

I raked over the grave and scattered debris and fallen branches over the area. Then we pushed the barrow and tools back to the yard. But just as I was stepping out of my tool shed, one of my neighbor Alain's twin sons came running onto the farm:

"Mr. Le Bras! Mr. Le Bras! German soldiers have taken my father away!"

I stared at him in disbelief. "What, when?" was all I could think to ask.

"This morning—my mother is crying and I don't know what to do. Can you please help?"

"What were the charges?" I asked.

But the boy just stared at me blankly, shaking his head.

Jacqueline came over and put her arm around the boy's narrow shoulders: "Go back and try to comfort your mother," she said. "Tell her we will do whatever we can to bring him home."

We took him back out to the road and sent him speeding on his way. And as we turned back to the *ti-annez*, Jacqueline again looked to me for counsel.

I sat on the porch steps and stared at the ground. Everything was happening much too fast. The world had turned upside down, and everybody, it seemed, wanted me to right it.

"Go to the German command post and try to talk to that sergeant," I said, finally. "Be nice to him and perhaps he will forgive you for biting his hand." We exchanged rueful smiles. "Let's see what he is willing to tell you."

"Good idea," she said. "They are probably housed in the same jail."

"At least for the time being," I agreed.

When Jacqueline left, I returned to the heath to make my peace with Ephraim. He wouldn't speak to me, so I locked him back up.

Then I went into Kérity to see Yann. I walked into his house filled with guilt, and when he greeted me with enthusiasm, I felt worse.

"Have you seen my father? He was looking for you."

"I haven't," I said. "I've just got into town. Why do you ask?"

"He was going to meet you by the boat. Someone broke into our fishing locker the other day, and he wanted to ask you about it."

If only he had, I thought. Aloud I said, "I didn't see him."

"He told me you and Jean-Pierre were going to cast the nets this morning. We thought that I would try to help bring them in. I was to meet him at the harbor at four. What do you suppose has happened?"

"Jean-Pierre was arrested by the Nazis yesterday. They also searched my house looking for Ephraim," I replied. "And this morning they arrested my neighbor Alain. Maybe they have your father, too."

Yann stared at me for a moment, and then nodded his head slowly. "But is there nothing we can do?" Then he turned to me once more. "Why didn't they arrest you?"

"I was lucky," I said. "I gave them some cider, and that seemed to be good enough. But as for the Jean-Pierre and Alain, Jacqueline is making inquiries. Let's wait till she gets back. In the meantime, let's go down to the harbor and repair that locker."

18

Three days later Jacqueline returned to the farm. She fell into my arms, laid her head on my shoulder and cried herself out. When she was finished, I sat her down on the porch and waited.

She stayed very still for some time, moving only to sip from the glass of cider I had poured. But then, when she had fully collected herself, she began to speak. "My first stop was Alain's farm, but I wasn't able to learn much."

"What were the charges?"

"Harboring an undesirable—Jeanne-Marie is beside herself with grief. But at least, as you said, Alain's arrest gave me a legitimate reason to go talk to Weber. He's been promoted, you know; he's a lieutenant now."

"I'm not surprised. They need officers who can speak French."

"But he has also become very arrogant. He acted as though I had missed a wonderful opportunity to become an officer's whore." She gave a hollow laugh.

"But what did you learn? Where were they keeping them? Are they together?"

Jacqueline nodded. "He told me they were in the police cells at Kemper for the time being, and he told me he would get them released if I would sleep with him."

"He said *what*?"

"You heard me; he said if I became his whore, he would do all he could to get them out. For a moment I even considered it. In fact, if he could have guaranteed their release, and that I only had to do it once, I might have said yes. But you know he would have held that over my head for the rest of the war. And I don't believe he has the authority to get Jean-Pierre released. Maybe Alain, but not Jean-Pierre. I doubt they will hold Alain very long, anyway."

"That makes sense. He's more useful to them working on his farm producing food. Besides, I don't think Alain was aware

Jean-Pierre was Jewish to begin with. They probably understand that. But I'm interrupting you. Please continue."

"I took the bus to Kemper, and it dropped me off beside the cathedral. From there it is just a short walk to the municipal cells. There is a cafe across the street, so I went in there and sat in a window where I could watch the door. But only civilians entered and left; there were no German uniforms anywhere. Half an hour later I went in to inquire after Alain.

"There were three men and two women in the offices, and I spoke to a girl named Solenn who looked and dressed like a local. It was a lucky choice. She works there as a secretary, and she told me to meet her in the cafe at lunchtime. She couldn't say much more. Apparently, the jail has been taken over by Vichy sympathizers.

"We had lunch together. She's a patriot, which is good, but she's very indiscreet, and if she isn't careful, she and her entire family will be arrested."

"What do you mean?" I asked.

Jacqueline sighed and shook her head. "Well, after we ordered our sandwiches and coffee, Solenn glanced furtively around the cafe, like a spy in a movie. It was so obvious. It was just lucky there were no Germans there watching. Padrig, you were right, people don't understand what can happen to them. Solenn will be lucky if she lasts another month. Anyway, she told me that all the department heads are minor bureaucrats who may or may not be collaborators. But the town's people for the most part sympathize with de Gaulle and the English.

"'Do you know that for a fact?' I asked, and she looked at me warily, as though she suddenly realized she didn't know if she could trust me. But I managed to reassure her that we were on the same side. 'How many Bretons are in the prison now?' I said, after she decided to trust me again.

"'There are four. Two are local men, and there are two more the Germans brought in the other day, although one of those is being released tomorrow.'

"'That must be Alain, my neighbor.'

"Solenn nodded. 'The others are going to Rennes later this week. Unless…' She gave me a little smile.

"'You mean something's going to happen?' I looked up with renewed interest.

"'Maybe,' she said. 'But I cannot tell you more.'

"But she had told me plenty already. 'Is there someone else to whom I can talk about this?' I said. 'We wouldn't want anything to happen before Alain is released. He has a wife and five children to support. He can't afford to go into hiding. But if there's going to be some sort of breakout, I should like to be sure our other friend is included.'

"Solenn nodded, pulled a scrap of paper from her pocket, and scribbled something on it. 'Go to this address and ask for Serge. He's my brother. Tell him what you told me.'

"After Solenn left the cafe to go back to work, I followed her directions through the cobbled streets to her tiny house. It was located along a dark and narrow alleyway down by the river. And as I walked to the door, I could hear someone moving around on the upper floor above my head. I knocked on the door and stepped back so I could see the upstairs windows. But the shuffling noise I heard previously had stopped. A few moments later a deep voice called out softly: 'Who's there?'

"'I'm a friend of Solenn. I have a message for Serge.'

"'Are you alone?'

"'Yes.'

"'Just a minute.'

"A few moments later the heavy oak door pulled back, and a middle-aged man, his face leathery and worn, poked his head outside. He was wearing a collarless shirt, a dark and tattered vest and on his head, pulled over to one side, was an old beret. He looked me over, glanced up and down the alley and then pulled me inside.

"'I've never seen you before. Who are you?'

"'I told you, I'm a friend of Solenn. My name's Jacqueline. Are you Serge?' He shook his head. 'Serge is not here. What do you want?'

"'My message is for his ears only. It's about the prisoners in the city jail.' The man's face remained expressionless. 'Listen,' I said. 'You can trust me. I'm a patriot. I've lived here for years. I speak Breton. Isn't that proof enough?'

"'All right then. Come with me. But let me warn you now, if you're not who you say you are, you'll be dead before nightfall. Do you understand?'

"I nodded, and he led me into a back room, where another man, this one considerably younger, sat behind a table facing the door.

"'I am Serge,' he said. 'What can I do for you?'

"'I understand that you intend to spring your friends out of jail,' I began. 'I just would like you to include another man, a friend of mine, when you do it. He's in the same cell, so it shouldn't be too difficult.'

"'What's he in for?'

"'He's being transported to Germany. He's a Jew. If we don't save him, he'll probably be dead within weeks.'

"He asked me a lot more questions, and we haggled back and forth a long time before he nodded his head wearily.

"'All right, Jacqueline. I'll do what I can, but I can't promise anything. You see, we're not going to break into the jail; we're going to derail the train to Rennes and pull our men from the wreckage. If your friend, what's his name—Jean-Pierre—if Jean-Pierre is on the train and the crash doesn't kill him, then fine, we'll take him, too. But I warn you, even if we do succeed, he will have to disappear into the *maquis*. So there won't be any way to get a message back to you. And if he's really lucky, we will eventually ship him across the English Channel to safety. But that's a big if.'

"This was Jean-Pierre's only chance, so I nodded my head and we shook hands. And just before I left the house, I asked Serge to tell Jean-Pierre that his child was safe. Then I caught the bus out of town before the evening curfew."

When Jacqueline finished her story, she closed her eyes wearily, and I filled her glass once more.

* * * *

Two days later a Nazi limousine carrying Leutnant Weber and followed by a truck-load of soldiers pulled onto my farm. And as soon as I saw them, I guessed the train to Rennes had been intercepted.

"*Guten morgan*, Herr Le Bras," said Weber, as he stepped out of his limo. "Is Mademoiselle de Bavière at home?"

"She doesn't live here," I replied. "She is back in her cottage on the Le Goff farm. Why do you ask?"

"I have to inform her that her friend, the Jew-boy, is dead, and I also need to ask her more questions."

I kept my face as deadpan as possible as I absorbed the shocking news. "He's dead?" I said. "How did he die?"

"The train taking him to Rennes derailed and crashed, and his guards, suspecting partisan sabotage, shot all three prisoners before they could escape."

"And Alain, was he on board, too?"

"No, he is being released soon, thanks to me. You can tell Mademoiselle de Bavière he is being freed due to my testimony. But for now, he's still in jail in Quimper."

And then with a triumphal smirk, Weber turned on his heels and stepped back into his limo.

19

As I watched the Nazi limousine pull off my property, I wondered why Weber would feel the need to bring so many soldiers with him if he simply wished to inform us of Jean-Pierre's death. But derailing the train to Rennes was the first significant local act of sabotage, and he probably planned to arrest Jacqueline or at least take her in for questioning. And of course. with her in his "protective" custody he could also work toward his other, more personal, objective.

Good luck with that, Herr Leutnant, I thought. That would be like trying to bed a lioness after slaughtering her cubs, and the result would be much the same.

But the gravity of the situation quickly wiped away this feeble attempt at gallows humor. Clearly Jacqueline was in danger, and if she were in custody, how long would it take Weber to link her to Jakez's disappearance? And then of course to me, my farmstead, and his grave. The way I saw it, we had to get her out of harm's way as soon as possible—and if that meant spiriting her away to England, so be it!

And then there was Ephraim. What would we do with him? I tried to think of a plan that would work. But each idea involved taking my responsibility to my lost friend and passing it on to someone else. Since I was planning a voyage to England anyway, and I had no idea how to get in touch with his mother in Paris, I should take Ephraim, too. He would finally be safe from harm and, more importantly to me, this was a solution I could live with.

* * * *

The next morning, when there was still no sign of Jacqueline, I guessed she had stayed with Jeanne-Marie or slept at Jean-Pierre's cabin, so I rode over there. Both women were sitting together in the main cottage. One would be receiving good news, the other devastating, but as I sat down beside them and they both looked to me, once again I felt entirely inadequate and unqualified to deal with these appalling and murderous times.

The hour that followed was very harrowing for us all. However, Jacqueline held herself together surprisingly well. But when I complimented her on her composure, she leapt up and ran sobbing from the room.

"Shall I go after her?" I said to Jeanne-Marie. But she was already on her feet shaking her head.

"It is better that I go," she said. "But do not leave, Padrig. Jacqueline has something to tell you too."

She then followed Jacqueline out the door, leaving me to wonder what that could possibly be. I learned soon enough—Jacqueline was with child. She implored me to help her prevent Jean-Pierre's baby from being born under the yoke of the invader.

* * * *

I sat them both down and outlined my plans. I told Jacqueline to take food and stay with Ephraim up on the heath until I had the *Kenavo* ready for our voyage.

"How long will that take?" said Jacqueline.

"It depends on the weather and of course any military activity in Kérity that might delay us—but hopefully, one or two nights. Jeanne-Marie will keep you fed and aware of all developments." I looked at Jeanne-Marie and she nodded her consent.

"And how long will the voyage take?"

"About fifteen hours. We have to be very careful as we sail around the French Atlantic coast, but the British Navy controls the English Channel, so once we are in those waters, we should be relatively safe."

Jacqueline nodded. "It's a great plan, Padrig, but what can we do about Weber?"

"I don't think we can do anything. Weber is not so bad; at least you can reason with him. And even if we could take him out, it would make little difference. He would be replaced in an instant by someone who could be a lot worse."

"Of course, you are right."

"Get yourself up on the heath and wait for word. I promise I will keep you informed."

* * * *

My next job was to persuade Yann into letting me take the *Kenavo* to England. Indeed, I needed him to help me. This was getting complicated. Would I really be able to pull this off? Even though the entire community was treating me as though I were the wise elder of Kérity, I had no answers. What did they expect? A year ago I was a simple peasant, fisherman, and raconteur. Hopelessness and guilt pressed down upon me as I rode into Kérity and to Yann's cottage.

As I dismounted and leaned my bicycle against a wall, Yann opened his door and stood beside it leaning on a makeshift crutch. At first glance he reminded me of an eighteenth-century English pirate. He was just missing the eye patch and parrot.

"My father still hasn't returned, and from what I hear, the Nazis haven't detained him. I went to the Village Hall and asked Anna. She hadn't heard a word about that. I'm getting worried; it's not like him to disappear without a word. Where could he have gone?"

I walked toward the cottage. "I have no idea," I said, lying through my teeth. "I need him, too." We went inside the cottage and sat at a small table. "Listen, Yann, beside your missing father, we have other problems, although they may be related. I really don't know."

I crossed myself to wash away my blatant lies. "A lot has happened in the last few days—none of it good. First, the Nazis arrested Jean-Pierre; someone told them he was a Jew. Then they arrested my neighbor Alain simply because Jean-Pierre was staying on his property." I paused.

Yann remained expressionless. "Where are they interred? There is no jail in Kérity."

"They were taken to Kemper, although Jean-Pierre was sent to Rennes on a train with two other prisoners suspected of resistance work and sabotage. But when the train was derailed by other Résistance fighters, the German guards shot the prisoners to prevent their escape."

Yann struggled to his feet, clutching the table. "Do you think my father was one of them?"

"I suppose it's possible," I said, "But Jean-Pierre was definitely one, and now I hear that Jacqueline is pregnant with his baby."

"Has she been arrested, too? She could also be accused of harboring a Jew. After all, she was living with him."

"She is still free as of now. I have her hidden up on the heath with Ephraim, but I think we should transport them both to England on the *Kenavo*. They will be safe there."

"Ephraim? Is he Jean-Pierre's son? I hear he is quite a handful."

"That is exactly why we have to take them to England. It would be impossible to hide him around here for the duration. This war could last for several more years."

"Do you need me to go with you? What about my father? I have to find him."

"I think you have to face the possibility that Jakez is either dead or in jail. There is really no other explanation. And I have an obligation to Jacqueline and Ephraim to get them to safety before they are arrested, too. Besides, we would only be gone a couple of days. If we are lucky, nothing much will have changed by the time we return."

"Then count me in," said Yann. "What is our next move?"

We shook hands solemnly across the table. *So far, so good*, I thought. Now all I have to do is persuade Jacqueline not to say anything on the boat about Yann's father's death.

"Let's sail down to Vannes," I replied. "I can check with the local Résistance there and see if there is any protocol we have to follow as we sail to England. If all goes well, when we return to Kérity, I will collect our passengers from the heath, and we can leave on the morning tide."

20

Our trip to Vannes, an important fishing port in the Gulf of Morbihan, was successful. I met with Hervé Riou, a deep-sea trawler captain who is also Alain and Jeanne-Marie's brother-in-law, and some other old fishermen friends. I came away with the information I needed—a time and coordinates to meet with an English fishing boat in the mouth of La Manche. Apparently this meeting, which often included an exchange of passengers going in either direction, had been in place for several weeks.

All I had to do now was to stop by my farmstead and retrieve my passengers. As I pedaled into my yard after we returned from Vannes, however, something was very wrong. The silence was profound and ominous, even songbirds were mute. Then I spotted Weber's motorcycle behind the cider barn.

I cautiously opened the kitchen door, and sitting at the table alone and half-naked was Jacqueline, her face buried in blood-stained hands. She turned toward me, her eyes both weary and sorrowful.

"Ephraim is still on the heath," she said, as she pulled a cloth across her breasts.

I said nothing at first, but I looked beyond her trembling body and saw Weber lying in the doorway with a large kitchen knife protruding from between his shoulder blades.

Jacqueline stood up carefully, clutching the table to steady herself. "If you do something about that," she said, pointing to the body, "I'll get dressed and fetch Ephraim down from the heath."

After another disgusted glance at Weber she continued. "He caught me taking food to Ephraim, so I had to distract him. Later, when he fell asleep after taking something he didn't deserve, I gave him something he did. I'll explain everything later, when we're safely out at sea." She then turned and stepped over the body to retrieve her clothes.

After she dressed, Jacqueline helped me load Weber into my wheelbarrow and then left to fetch Ephraim from the heath. And by the time I had finished burying him and his motorcycle they were back—Jacqueline strong and determined, and Ephraim sullen but quiet.

"He knows about his father," she said. "But he hasn't said a word since I told him, although he hasn't been difficult."

"Does he know where we are taking him?"

"Just that it's somewhere safe; a land where there are no Nazi rapists," she replied, her voice still tinged with outrage.

* * * *

A half-hour before dawn two days later, the *Kenavo* met with a Brixham trawler in the mouth of the English Channel, and we transferred Ephraim and Jacqueline to the crew. I was happy to see them safely on board, although I guessed we would be returning to a firestorm in Kérity, thanks to Weber's disappearance.

We decided not to return immediately, but to drop anchor in Vannes and make some inquiries. And I learned that the Nazi command had wreaked instant and terrible vengeance on Kérity and its people, most of whom I had known all my life.

They marched onto Alain's farm and executed not only Alain, but his twelve-year-old twin boys. They had put them up against the wall of Jean-Pierre's cottage and shot them in front of Jeanne-Marie and their three remaining children: two young girls, Annette and Chantal, and their youngest son, Fernand. They also executed several other of Kérity's more prominent citizens.

Needless to say, when we finally returned, we were not popular. Jacqueline was condemned as a Nazi officer's slut and the betrayer of Jean-Pierre, and we were blamed for spiriting her away and leaving the town to bear the brunt of the Nazi revenge.

And that, Tommy, as depressing as it is, is the story of your mother's life in Kérity. I hope this helps you in your quest to understand her.

21

Tommy Kiernan
Kérity, France—May 1959

I leaned back and closed my eyes as Padrig's extraordinary account of my mother's wartime perils came to a conclusion. What a tale of survival! But of course it didn't end there for either Padrig or me. He still had to navigate his way through a brutal war in German-occupied France with the bodies of two of the story's principal players—the Nazi officer Weber and his disgraced friend Jakez—buried on his property.

But simply the fact that twenty years later he was still fishing with Jakez's son, and after a difficult day on the ocean was able to recount a compelling, heart-stopping history, was proof positive that my mother's old friend and contemporary was also the ultimate survivor. And I had to cope with the revelation that my sweet, but tight-lipped mother was ready and able to dispense immediate and lethal justice whenever it was necessary.

Then there was the child who arrived in Brixham with my mother. He was not only my half-brother, but he also hated her for displacing his mother in his father's affections. What had happened to this boy, this Ephraim Goldfeldt? Did he still harbor those feelings of hatred twenty years later?

Where did I go from here? At this point I had no idea—but there were also more and equally urgent questions to occupy my mind. "Did you ever tell Yann how and why his father was killed?"

"The truth, you mean? No, I never did. It's better this way. I told him that when I went home to pick up Jacqueline and Ephraim, I found Jacqueline in a state of utter shock, and both Weber and Jakez dead, and that was all I knew. This gives him an honorable epitaph, and I'm happy to leave it that way."

"But did Yann accept that? Didn't Jacqueline tell him the facts?"

"No, she wasn't going to implicate herself in two murders. She simply told young Yann that Weber raped her multiple times, and she eventually passed out. She was just coming to when I found her, and we guessed that your father and Weber killed each other. Your father had been shot, and Weber stabbed with a kitchen knife. And I buried them both in the woods beyond my property."

"And Yann was satisfied with that explanation?"

"I think so; he didn't question me, and he certainly did not believe that Jacqueline was a Nazi officer's slut and collaborator. This is not the opinion of all my friends. For instance, Jeanne-Marie and her surviving children still blame her for the destruction of their family."

"I can understand why—that was a barbaric act, even by war-time standards. But I would still like to talk to her," I said. "Do you know where she is now?"

"I don't. We are no longer friends—she still partially blames me for her loss, too. She doesn't live here anymore, but her two daughters are married and living and working the farm with their spouses."

"Would you take me to meet them? If they knew my mother and especially if they remember Ephraim Goldfeldt, I really need to speak with them. But first, of course, I need to find somewhere to stay. Can you recommend lodgings?"

"The Auberge du Pont would be perfect. That is where I encountered both your mother and your father, and also where they met each other. Do you have luggage?"

"I left a bag at the train station, and I noticed a sign there for taxi service. That will get me to the *auberge*. Can I meet you there and continue our conversation?"

"It is getting late, Tommy. I'll come to the *auberge* tomorrow at noon and we can continue then." He rose to his feet and held out his hand. "*Kenavo*, Tommy, until tomorrow."

* * * *

Over lunch at the *auberge*, Padrig told me he could take me to Alain's farm if I insisted, but he added a warning: "I don't think you will be welcome. The girls seem to have forgiven me, but they still blame your mother for the executions."

"It's terrible that they still hold a grudge against my mother for Nazi atrocities that took place twenty years ago. But it's understandable."

"Yes, they all have long memories, and they are furious that she escaped to England, leaving their family to bear the brunt of the Nazi fury—especially the cold-blooded assassination of the twins. As I told you earlier, they forced Jeanne-Marie and the small children to watch the executions."

"Oh, my God!" I said, horrified. "How many children were there again?"

"Two girls, Annette and Chantal. They still work the farm with their husbands, and a little boy, Fernand. Fernand went away to school, and the last I heard, he was taking graduate courses at a law school in America. He has become the pride of the family."

Jeanne-Marie has a son living in America? That's an interesting coincidence, I thought. Aloud I said: "Will you take me to their farm this afternoon?"

"Of course I will."

"Do they speak French? I don't speak Breton."

"Since the war all Breton children have learned French in school. Indeed, your mother was Alain's children's first teacher. They will answer you in French—if they speak to you at all."

22

"*Bonjour*, Chantal," said Padrig, as the farmhouse door opened slowly to reveal a young woman in a rumpled house coat with a baby under her arm.

"Padrig, I haven't seen you in a while. How have you been?" Chantal replied. "And who is this young man? He looks familiar." She glanced at me and gave me a fleeting smile.

"Let me introduce Tommy Kiernan," Padrig continued. "He is an American, come to seek his roots here in Brittany." Padrig nodded in my direction. "This is my neighbor, Chantal Boucher, whom I have known since she was a baby. She is the daughter of dear friends."

"What can I do for you, Monsieur?" said Chantal, looking directly at me.

"*Bonjour*, Madame; please call me Tommy. And as Padrig mentioned, I come from America to France searching for traces of my parents, whom I'm told met here in Kérity. My mother came here in the thirties to train as an artist. She also worked here as a teacher of the French language. Her name was Jacqueline de Bavière. I am told my father was Jean-Pierre Goldfeldt, a Parisian journalist who came here to work on a book of Breton tales and legends. They stayed for a while at a cottage on this farm. Do you remember them?"

As soon as my parent's names registered with the young woman, her face hardened, her eyes narrowed, and she attempted to slam the door in our faces. Padrig, however, thrust his boot across the threshold.

"Please, Madame, hear me out," I pleaded. "I have traveled several thousand miles to learn my mother's story. Surely you can allow me fifteen minutes?"

"Jacqueline de Bavière was directly responsible for the destruction of my family. I despise her very name—our entire family does."

"Do you not believe the Nazi executioners are more deserving of your hatred than Jacqueline, Chantal?" said Padrig. "For the love of God, let the boy speak."

The woman turned back to me reluctantly. "What is your business here?"

"Thank you for your indulgence, Madame. I'm here to learn all I can of my mother and father's early life."

"All I know is what my mother told me, and she believed Jacqueline betrayed her country by not only collaborating with the Nazis but sharing a Nazi officer's bed. It was Jacqueline, my mother said, who informed him of the Jewish refugee we were hiding on our farm. This Nazi officer, Leutnant Weber, is in all probability the missing birth father of whom you speak," the woman added, giving me a withering look as she hitched up her baby and once again attempted to slam shut the door.

"Chantal, Chantal…" said Padrig. "That is not at all the truth. Please listen to us. I was there, too, and we weren't just hiding a Jewish journalist, but also his son. Surely you remember Ephraim?"

Chantal nodded reluctantly and opened the door wide enough to allow us to enter. She then led us to a small room where a rough-hewn table and several chairs sat in a corner. On the wall behind the table was a painting of the farmyard outside with three young boys playing around an ancient plow—a painting in a style that looked tantalizingly familiar. Was it one of my mother's? And if so, had I seen it before?

Chantal motioned toward the chairs, and when we took our seats, she sat across from us and began breast-feeding her baby as though it were the most normal thing in the world and Padrig and I didn't exist.

My eyes immediately fixed on the painting.

"This story, as you tell it, Chantal," said Padrig, completely ignoring her bared bosom, "is not remotely close to the truth. The Nazi officer was not her lover, he was her rapist, and he paid the ultimate price for his actions. I know because the attack occurred at my homestead while I was away. Fortunately, however, he was interrupted by a family friend, my fishing partner Jakez. You must remember Jakez. Well, it seems the two men killed each other. Jakez was shot and the Nazi was stabbed, and Jacqueline was in a state of shock. That is how I found them when I returned that morning. And because it was no longer possible for Jacqueline to remain safely in Kérity, Jakez's son Yann and I spirited her and the boy Ephraim away to England in Jakez's fishing boat as soon as we could possibly arrange it."

"That is not how it was told to me," said Chantal. "I was here with the rest of my family when soldiers stormed onto the farm and slaughtered my father and my brothers. Right there against that wall. The twins were barely twelve." Chantal's face still showed the horror of that moment as she pointed out through a window to the cottage wall and the brass plaque mounted upon it, which began: "*Mort pour la France…*"

Padrig and I stood in silent homage as we stared out through the window at the plaque, a monument to lives senselessly destroyed.

I then turned back to Chantal, whose eyes were now wet with tears. "I am eternally sorry for your loss, Madame, but my mother was not responsible for such a barbaric act. It was Nazis who shot them, after all."

"But what can I do for you now, after all these years, Monsieur," she said as she moved her baby from one breast to the other.

"Madame, Padrig recently explained to me that my parents were friends of your parents, and my mother was quite possibly your first tutor in the French language. Well, she recently died in an automobile accident, and I am attempting of learn as much about her life as I possibly can." I smiled at my reluctant hostess. "I'm thinking of writing a biography of her life. She was a very accomplished artist, as I am sure you know. I believe you have one of her paintings on the wall behind you."

"That painting has hung there for as long as I remember," she replied. "I have no idea who the artist was."

"I don't know for sure, but I believe it is one of my mother's."

Now I remembered why it seemed so familiar; there was a sketch just like it in Jackie's journal: three boys playing in a farm-yard.

Meanwhile Padrig's eyes were drawn to the painting, and he walked over and examined it. "Those are your twin brothers and Jean-Pierre's son Ephraim in the painting," he said.

"If you say so, Padrig; you must understand I was very young during the war."

"It was horrendous time for all of us," I said. "I was born in England in 1940, and I dodged bombs and slept in air-raid shelters for five long, painful years. Of course, it was much worse for you, losing your father and your brothers. But is it fair to blame my mother because France was at war with Germany? She was a victim of the times, as were your parents and your siblings."

"My mother remembers Jacqueline as a Nazi officer's slut and a collaborator—a collaborator who was directly responsible for the death of my father and my two brothers. That is all I know or wish to know."

"Well, Madame, I spent the other evening with Padrig here, and he tells a much different story—a story of my mother's hatred of the Nazis and of her active resistance, and how she was constantly trying to recruit Padrig into taking a stand against them."

The baby finished her lunch and Chantal adjusted her housedress and deposited her on the floor. "The fact remains, Monsieur, I was no more than six years old when I last saw your mother. I do not understand how I can be of any assistance to you. I am not even sure what you hope to gain by being here and bringing back memories of those terrible times and of my murdered father and brothers."

"I want to change the negative opinion you all have of Jacqueline de Bavière. She was a wonderful mother, and it is very painful to hear her described as a slut and a Nazi collaborator," I said. I rose from my chair and studied the painting. "Does your mother own this picture? I am thinking of gathering a collection of her works and would like to buy it. Would you take me to meet her?"

"I do not think she wants to see you or sell the painting. It is the only image we have of the twins. But I will tell her of your interest. How much would you be willing to pay?"

"I have no wish to haggle with honest people, especially since you have suffered so much. I would bring an expert to appraise the painting and I would pay the fair market price. I would also have it professionally photographed, enlarged, and framed to present to you as a replacement. This way you would not lose your only image of your brothers."

Chantal gave me the first genuine smile of our encounter. "That is very fair, Monsieur, and I shall convey your message to my mother. Are you staying locally? How can I find you again?"

"For now, Madame, I am staying at the Auberge du Pont. I will, however, soon be heading to Paris to attempt to find my mother's family. I believe her father was a wine trader in a small town named Senlis north of Paris during the thirties."

"Will you be returning to Brittany after your visit?" She stood.

"Yes, indeed, I expect to return soon. I am not anticipating a warm welcome by my mother's family. I believe they disowned her after she moved to Brittany to pursue her dream. I simply want to tell them that she is dead."

She walked with us to the door. "Then I'll write to my mother and tell Padrig if she decides to speak to you, but do not be too optimistic; *kenavo*, Tommy; *kenavo*, Padrig."

Chantal closed the farm door behind us, and Padrig and I walked back up the road toward his farmstead.

"A somewhat successful visit, Tommy, under the circumstances," said Padrig. "What do you think?"

"Chantal seems to be a reasonable woman." I replied. "I think she will come around. But what of the rest of the family—her sister and brother? Do you think their mother has permanently poisoned their minds against Jacqueline? And then there's the painting. Was it a gift from my mother?"

"I'm sure it was. But it's the only likeness Jeanne-Marie has of the twins, and for that reason I don't know if she would sell it."

"You could right," I replied. "But I have a friend who is an art appraiser, and she believes that Jacqueline's work is quite valuable. I'm sure they could use the money."

We reached Padrig's farmstead and he waved me to a chair on the porch. He then walked across the courtyard toward the barn with the cider press—as he must have done a thousand times before for his guests, expected and otherwise.

While he was in the barn, I imagined my birth father as he was in 1939, when he first came to Brittany to collaborate with Padrig on that book of Breton tales and legends. I imagined further the moment when the three artists—the painter, the writer, and the raconteur—first met in conversation all those years ago at the

Auberge du Pont. It might have been a truly historic moment in the art world, if it hadn't been wiped out by the war.

"You seem to be lost in your thoughts, Tommy," said Padrig, as he handed me a brimming ceramic cider pot. "Where are they, my friend, far away or here in the land of your roots?"

"They are not so far away, Padrig. I am trying to imagine the artistic thoughts and ideas that came up in conversation when you first met with Jacqueline and Jean-Pierre at the Auberge."

"It was quite a meeting, I can tell you. And among the other thoughts and ideas, I am quite sure that the seeds of *Fishermen of Kérity* came from that conversation."

I smiled at Padrig. "You know, I've matured beyond my years in the few days I have known you."

23

I returned to Brittany from Senlis a week later. My meeting with my grandparents was neither happy nor useful. Jacqueline's father, now an old man confined to a wheelchair, was only interested in his daughter and the news of her death when I mentioned that her paintings might have some value.

Her mother said very little from the moment I introduced myself to her as her grandson. She simply stared at me constantly, as if to wonder who I was and what was I doing here. I didn't stay. I took my rental car and headed west.

But what had I learned? Who hated my mother enough to travel to America to kill her? Indeed, who even knew she was there?

Had she kept in touch with Ephraim? It wasn't likely, since according to both Padrig and my father, or rather my step-father, Frank, they detested one another. But how would I find him? Should I go to Brixham? Was it possible he was still there?

I arrived at the harbor just as Yann and Padrig were stowing their nets.

"Let's go to L'Etoile," I said. "I have a request." And after we were sitting around the table in what had become my favorite spot in town—I told them I needed to go to Brixham.

"Brixham," said Yann. "What's in Brixham?"

"I don't know," I replied. "But I was born there and lived there for several years when I was a young child. I don't remember Ephraim's name ever being mentioned, but it's the only link I have to him, and I need to find him. I'd be willing to pay you for the voyage."

"Oh no, that isn't necessary," said Padrig. "Of course we will take you and bring you back. We take locally grown vegetables over there all the time. Not just to Brixham, but all along the English coast. We sell them in the markets and even door to door sometimes. It pays the bills and it's good for the local farmers. We can sell produce while you search for Ephraim."

"A perfect solution," I said. "When can we leave?"

* * * *

Two days later the *Kenavo* sailed around Berry Head. The large promontory juts into the sea and shelters Brixham from the storms that race in from the west every fall. As I stood in the bow beside the bags of produce admiring both the harbor and the town terraced above and around it, I planned my first steps.

I found my way to the parish church and knocked on the rectory door. "Good afternoon," I said to the lady who answered. "I am not sure at all that I'm at the right place, but my half-brother, whom I do not know, was a refugee from France brought to Brixham as a boy during the early days of World War II and I am trying to trace him. Do you have any idea to where he might have been taken?"

The woman, a tall, well-dressed lady probably in her fifties, stared at me blankly for a moment before ushering me into the house and into a drawing room. "Won't you please sit down, Mr. er…"

"Tommy Kiernan, but please call me Tommy," I said.

"Very well, Tommy," she replied with a pleasant country drawl. "Do you know when your brother arrived here?"

"As a matter of fact, I do, but that's about all I know: it was the summer of 1940."

"Ah," she said. "Not long after the Germans overran France. How old was he at the time?"

"I think nine or ten; his parents were killed by the Nazis."

"I hope you don't mind me asking you this, but if his parents were killed by the Nazis, how is he your brother? You are much too young."

"It's a long story," I said, as I told her of my mother, her death, my father's death and my quest to find an answer. In the meantime, an outside door opened and closed, and when I finished my story, the vicar's wife went to the hallway and called her husband in. "Gerald darling, come into the drawing room if you please. We have a guest."

And after she made the introductions, she told her husband of my quest.

The Reverend Brougham, a tall, imposing man, even taller than his wife, with his black suit and white dog collar, smiled at me kindly.

"I was a young deacon here in 1940, newly ordained and full of vim and vigor," he said. "If you can wait, I can ring a friend who was on the refugee committee at the time. I joined the committee the following year, so I wouldn't remember your mother or your brother. Would you care for something to eat and drink? Eleanor, my dear, would you ask Joan to put on the kettle?" With that he stepped back out to the hall and the telephone.

A pot of tea and biscuits, with cups and saucers so delicate I was almost afraid to touch them, had been served by the time the vicar returned, some fifteen minutes later.

"I have news, some good and some less so," he said. "Do you know West Norwood or Worthing at all?"

"I'm afraid not," I said. "I was born in Brixham and lived here until 1950 when my family immigrated to America, but we didn't travel much while we were here. Why, what's in West Norwood?"

"Norwood is a home for Jewish orphans. It's in the East End of London, and that's where Ephraim was originally sent. But when I rang them, I learned that the children were then evacuated to Worthing to be safe from the bombing. Ephraim was adopted by a Jewish-American army officer before the children returned to Norwood after the war. Unfortunately, they have no records of who this person was or where Ephraim was taken. I am sorry I cannot be of more help."

"Thank you for trying anyway, Reverend. Do you know where that other town is?"

"Worthing, you mean? It's on the south coast, east of here; it's about fifty miles directly south of London."

And, after thanking them both for their hospitality and their information, I made my way back to the harbor.

* * * *

On our return journey to Kérity, Padrig told me where to find Jeanne-Marie: "Chantal told me that she has moved in with her sister Adèle, the wife of Hervé Riou, a deep-sea trawler captain. She lives on the Ile de Conleau in the Golfe du Morbihan. It's just below Vannes, three kilometers south of the harbor there. Evidently their brother, who lives and works in the USA, is visiting, and he persuaded Jeanne-Marie to meet with you."

"Oh yes," I said, "the brother who lives in America. Where in America, do you know?"

"You can ask her yourself; although he will be gone by the time you arrive. His name is Fernand."

"And how old was he when his father and brothers were executed?"

"Maybe five or six, seven at the most. What are you implying? You will find that Fernand is a wonderful boy, and very good to his family."

"I'm implying nothing, Padrig, I'm merely thinking out loud. But if he witnessed the killings, and then listened to hateful tirades against my mother, that might have persuaded him to do something about it; even if it was simply to please his mother."

"But didn't you tell me there is no proof she was murdered, and that there was no one you knew who disliked her enough to want her dead?"

"That is true, Padrig. Her life in England and America was calm, almost boring, compared to life in Kérity. But the summer before she died, someone set fire to our house while we were sleeping. He was never caught. That is why her death seems so suspicious to me, and why I came here looking for you. And although it was no fault of my mother's, the whole of Kérity suffered—and blamed her for that suffering—after she killed Weber. This means that there are several possible suspects, don't you think? Anyway, I'll go to Vannes as soon as I can arrange it."

* * * *

Since I wasn't familiar with Vannes, I stopped at the harbor master's office and picked up a visitor's brochure. This told me that Vannes, or Gwened in Breton, is a walled port city located at the bottom of the Gulf of Morbihan. This large inland sea is dotted with tiny islands, and Conleau is one of only three or four with thriving communities. Vannes and Conleau are connected by a bridge situated just south of Vannes' bustling harbor, which itself is just outside the Gate of St. Vincent, one of the entrances through the massive walls that still surround the old town.

I stopped briefly to fortify myself with a shot of whiskey. I needed the courage before meeting former friends of my mother, women who nonetheless despised her and the memory of her since before I was born. I hesitated, then knocked on the door.

"And you are?" said a middle-aged woman suspiciously as she peered through the crack in the door. I had decided to be as open and truthful as possible and let the cards fall where they may.

"*Bonjour, Madame*," I said. "Am I addressing Madame Jeanne-Marie Le Goff?"

The door opened a little wider, and the woman nodded her head.

"My name is Tommy Kiernan, and I am the child of Jean-Pierre Goldfeldt and Jacqueline de Bavière."

She studied my face. "When I was told of your existence," she said, "I assumed your father was the Nazi Weber, but now I see a resemblance to Jean-Pierre. God save his soul!" The woman crossed herself and bent her head in silent prayer.

"They were terrible times," said I, pressing my advantage. "Times during which no family escaped unscathed—even my mother's."

"Your mother wished for nothing more than to make the world a better place. But in Kérity in 1940, ruled as we were by the forces of evil, I always feared her beauty and her wishes would cause more harm than good. Please, Monsieur Tommy, please come in and meet my sister." Jeanne-Marie finally opened the door and led me into a small but tidy parlor, where a woman sat beside a stone fireplace watching me intently.

"*Bonjour, Monsieur*," she said.

I replied politely and asked if she spoke French.

"Yes, of course," she said. "Your mother was our first French teacher. I am so sorry to hear of her unfortunate demise."

I explained my life with my mother and how, after she died, I found evidence of her life in France before and during the war. I was investigating to see if the circumstances of that life somehow contributed to her death.

"And now," I continued. "I learn that her former landlord, your brother-in-law Alain, was brutally murdered for sheltering her and her Jewish lover Jean-Pierre Goldfeldt—my birth father. I am here to offer my belated but sincere condolences, and more importantly to your sister—and my heartfelt thanks to her for sheltering my parents all those years ago."

When I turned back to Jeanne-Marie, she had tears in her eyes.

"All these years I blamed your mother for Alain's death," she stammered through her tears, "and that of my beautiful twin boys—those poor innocent boys. I can see now that I was wrong. It was those Nazi pigs. What have I done? What have we done?" Jeanne-Marie wept in her sister's arms.

"You have done nothing wrong, Jeanne-Marie," Adèle said. "This young man is here to offer his condolences—nothing more. We should accept them with our thanks and treat him as a guest— an honored guest—come back to us from the past."

"If only that were true," Jeanne-Marie said.

"Your presence here brings back very vivid and terrible memories of Alain's murder," said her sister. "His murder, Monsieur, whether you wish to believe it or not, was caused directly or indirectly by your mother's actions. Perhaps you should leave now and allow us to mourn our losses in private."

I shook my head. "I came to France to learn if there is any connection with my mother's life and actions in Brittany to her death in the United States. I am not going anywhere until I am satisfied that neither she nor you, for that matter, had anything to do with her death."

"My sister does not drive nor has she ever left Brittany. How could she possibly be involved with your mother's unfortunate car accident?"

I looked quickly at Jeanne-Marie and her sister. Did she really say that? "How do you know how she died?" I said. "I didn't tell you."

The two sisters glanced at each other silently. "I'm sure Chantal must have mentioned it in her letter. Yes, yes, that must have been it," said Jeanne-Marie, shrugging it off. "How else could I have possibly known?"

She turned back to her sister, leaving me with another unanswered question. Did I tell Chantal how my mother died?

I decided not to pursue the subject. If Fernand ran my mother off the road, then maybe he mentioned the accident to his mother on his last visit a few weeks ago. In the States I could inform my suspicions to the local police and have him investigated, and if he was guilty of causing my mother's accident, arrested.

"I apologize for upsetting you," I said.

Jeanne-Marie lifted her head. "Will you be returning to America soon, Tommy?"

"I haven't thought about my departure yet. But for now I'll return to Kérity. There is a painting at your farm that was, I believe, painted by my mother. I should like to buy it. Does it belong to you, Madame? It depicts your twin boys and my half-brother Ephraim."

"Chantal wrote to me about that. I accept your offer, including the photograph replacement. Do you know the appraisal amount?"

"No, but an art appraiser who is very familiar with my mother's work is coming over from America to appraise it. She will arrive in Cherbourg two days from now."

24

As I waited on the dock in Cherbourg watching the ocean liner *SS United States* slide into its berth, I felt great warmth for Genna—my friend, benefactor and even perhaps surrogate mother. Although I'm sure she would cringe at the thought of having an eighteen-year-old son, there was no denying my life and fortunes had changed for the better the moment we joined forces.

The ship's passengers began disembarking at one o'clock, which gave us a good reason to have a long lunch while I brought her up to date with my discoveries and suspicions.

"My God, Tommy," she said when I was almost finished. "You have already discovered enough material to fill a book. Not to mention two possible murder suspects—both of whom might be living in the United States. But how are you going to track them down?"

"It won't be difficult to find Fernand. I have several leads: I know his name, his profession, and also his favorite hobby. He spends most of his free time hiking in mountain ranges."

"That's chilling. Jacqueline died in the mountains."

"I had the same thought."

"And of course, if you didn't tell Chantal how your mother died, how would they know it was a car accident?" said Genna as she lifted her wine glass. "But what about Ephraim? He's going to be a lot more difficult to find."

"Yes, I know. I don't even know where to start."

"Did you think of going to that other town? What was it called?"

"Worthing, you mean?"

"Yes, what do you know about Worthing?"

"According to people I met in Brixham, Worthing is a seaside resort south of London. That's about all I know."

"Let's stop there on our way back. After all, you never know what you will find."

"If you don't mind, that would be great."

Genna laughed. "Of course I don't mind; just so long as you don't expect me to go there on a fishing boat. Oh, this is something that would interest you; a few days ago I was working in Jackie's studio, when there was a knock on the door. And when I opened it, a very attractive young lady stood outside. And when I asked if she was a friend of yours, she said, 'Not yet, but I hope to be. Is he here?'"

"'That's a very intriguing opening to a conversation, my dear,' I said. 'Come on in and tell me more.'

"So I brought her inside, sat at the table, and she told me this remarkable story of how you and she met in a cemetery at the college. Do you know who I'm talking about, Tommy?"

"I think so. I mean, I hope so: Was her name Adriana? I can't believe she found her way to the studio."

"Well, she did, and she's beautiful, to boot. I know you're only eighteen, but she seems like a keeper. Her name is Adriana Baker, and when I told her I was meeting with you in France, she asked me to give you this letter." Genna pulled an envelope from her purse and dropped it in front of me on the table. She shook her head when I reached for the letter. "You can read that later, but right now tell me about this painting I've come to see."

"It's a farmyard scene with three young boys playing around a plow. It's very good and I'm sure it's one of my mother's."

"If it is, it might fit right in with the exhibition I'm contemplating."

"The what?"

"I think Jackie's work deserves more exposure, don't you? A small exhibition that we could move from gallery to gallery would do the job perfectly."

* * * *

Padrig was the last to arrive. He insisted he always walked from his homestead to Alain's farm, and there was no reason to change his habits simply because I had rented a car. Jeanne-Marie and Adèle had arrived the evening before, and Genna and I arrived with Yann, who Padrig requested should also attend, exactly at noon.

I had brought Genna to the farm several days before to view the painting, and she spent the following day calling friends and acquaintances in the art world in New York, London, and Paris.

In the meantime, I arranged for a photographer from Quimper to take a picture of the barnyard painting, enlarge it and frame it, as my personal gift to Jeanne-Marie and her family.

At twelve-thirty, Padrig pulled himself to his feet and called the meeting to order. He then, in a surprising move, asked everyone to stand for a moment of silence to remember the departed.

"We who stand here today all survived a cruel and merciless war," he said, "during which we suffered devastating losses—fathers, mothers, friends; even beloved children and siblings. But now, my friends, now is the time to put away our suffering, our petty grudges, and come together with our relationships restored and reawakened."

Padrig then took my hand and brought me to Jeanne-Marie, and as we hugged each other in the center of the room, everyone clapped and even clasped their neighbor to them.

When order was restored, I presented Chantal with the framed photograph of my mother's painting and Genna's check for $15,000, which in post-war Brittany was untold wealth. It would help transform the Le Goff farm into a prosperous concern. She, in turn, unhooked the painting from the wall and gave it to me.

"Take care of my brothers," she said. "I still miss them desperately. Do you know what happened to Ephraim?"

"I only know he was adopted by an American army officer at the end of the war and taken to America, but I don't know where he lives," I replied.

That evening Genna and I hosted a dinner for everyone at the Auberge, during which I sat with Genna on one side and Yann on the other. Genna peppered him with questions about how a determined one-legged man became one of the most successful fishermen on the Atlantic Coast.

Yann believed his inspiration came from Padrig, his greatest supporter and a surrogate father when he'd needed one the most.

I couldn't have agreed more and got to my feet to offer a toast.

"To Padrig," I said as I raised my glass. "Whose strength and determination in the face of great odds has saved us all. He was a friend and loyal neighbor to the Le Goff family for many years; he brought Yann back from the dead and showed him he could still be a successful fisherman, and to me he has given a lasting picture of my parents and their all too brief life together."

* * * *

After the dinner, Jeanne-Marie and her family went back to their farm, while I took both Yann and Padrig back to their respective homes. And although they spoke quietly together in Breton, I gathered they were already planning their next day on the ocean.

"*Excusez moi*," I said, breaking into their conversation. "I'll be returning to America soon, where I'll be going back to school. But before I do, I would like to understand my father's work as a fisherman in Kérity. Would you take me fishing with you on the *Kenavo* tomorrow, or at least someday before I return to America?"

Yann and Padrig looked at each other and laughed. "In truth, Tommy," Padrig said. "We were wondering when you would ask."

"You will have to look the part, though," added Yann. "I think my father's black-peaked sailing cap would look great on you. What do you say, Padrig?"

"Show Yann the *Fishermen of Kérity* photograph, Tommy." Padrig turned to Yann. "I'm sure Tommy would like to look just like his father did in that picture. Is that possible?"

"I'll see what I can do," said Yann as he clambered out of the car by his home. "*Kenavo*, Tommy."

* * * *

When I returned to the Auberge, Genna was waiting at the bar.

"Mission accomplished," she said as I slid onto the stool beside her. "I believe we can go home now. Well, maybe not now, but in a day or two. We can take the ferry to England and Worthing and pick up the ship to New York in Southampton."

"Are you sure? Because I'm not. There may be other Bretons whose relatives were massacred after my mother escaped to England."

"Did Padrig mention anyone else?"

"No, but I am going out on the *Kenavo* tomorrow, and I'll discuss it with him then. If there are no other suspects, I guess we can go."

"You're going fishing tomorrow? I'm sure you'll enjoy that. Your only problem might be if you get seasick."

"I'll be fine; I wasn't sick when we sailed over to Brixham. Good night Genna; I'll see you in the morning."

Back in my room a few minutes later, I pulled Adriana's letter out of my coat pocket. We would be heading home in a few days and it would be good if my reply arrived at Middlebury before I did.

I read her words again:

Dear Tommy,

First of all, please allow me to offer you my deepest sympathies for the sudden and terrible loss of your mother. Your roommate Bill indicated that it was possibly murder. How awful! And of course you had to leave before we were able to meet properly, and before I could tell you in person how sorry I am. I wish you Godspeed and good luck with everything you are trying to discover. This was part of the reason I was looking for you; although if I am being truly honest, there was a selfish reason, too.

You see, I liked meeting you that day, and I resolved to visit the family gravesite every morning until I could run into you again. And that was how I met Bill several days later. He told me about your troubles and how I might find you, and when I finally got to your mother's studio, your friend Genna was there. She told me as much as she knew, too, and when she mentioned she was meeting you in France shortly, I scribbled these words for her to give to you.

Bill also told me you were perplexed by the gravesite I was tending. And although I'm sure it looked a little strange, the explanation is quite simple. My family on my mother's side comes from Middlebury, and my grandmother still lives there. I am staying with her as I attend the college to save the cost of staying on campus. The grave was that of her twin sister who died when she was only one, some seventy years ago. The day we met was their birthday.

Genna also told me that you intend to return to Middle-bury very shortly, and I am very much looking forward to meeting you properly and having that cup of hot chocolate.

Best wishes and continued luck in your endeavors, and I very much hope we can become friends,

Adriana Baker xxx

I kissed those tiny x's for the umpteenth time before writing my reply.

25

Worthing Central train station was quite large and busy, which surprised us. We hadn't realized Worthing was such a large town. And as we stepped onto the street, Genna immediately pointed to a taxi stand.

"Taxi drivers know everything there is to know about their district. See those men there?" She pointed to two men leaning against their cabs, puffing cigarettes. "Fountains of knowledge. You'll see." We walked over to them.

"Good morning, Madam," the older driver said as he pulled open his cab door. "Where are you headed?"

"Is there a synagogue in Worthing?"

"I don't know about that," he replied. He turned to his companion. "Bert, do you know of a synagogue here?"

"No, but I do have a regular fare, an elderly lady, Mrs. Cohen, who goes to a private house on Heene Road for a service every Saturday. Would you like to go there?"

Genna looked at me and smiled. "I told you." To the driver Bert, she said: "Take us away, Bert. It's as good a place to start as any."

As soon as we pulled away from the curb, Genna asked the driver how long he had driven a cab.

"Since the war, Madam; I know the best jobs are in construction, but I have a body full of shrapnel, so driving a cab seemed like a better idea."

"And Mrs. Cohen, how long have you been taking her to this house?"

"She was one of my first regular fares, Madam. During the war a group of Jews got together to help evacuate some orphaned children from a home in London."

"Maybe we should go see Mrs. Cohen," I said, as I explained our mission to Bert. "What do you think?"

"Oh, I think you should try Heene Road first. Mrs. Cohen is quite elderly and a little hard of hearing. You'll get more joy from Mr. Steener, the gent that owns the house where they gather. He's only about sixty."

Bert pulled up outside an imposing Edwardian mansion. "Would you like me to wait?" he said as he opened our door and indicated the house. "If Mr. Steener isn't there, I can take you to Mrs. Cohen's place."

"That would be great," said Genna. "I hope we won't be too long."

The door was answered by a maid, who immediately fetched a well-dressed older gentleman.

"Come in, come in," he said, as he showed us into the parlor. "To what do I owe this honor?"

"We're sorry to bother you, but we understand that religious services are held here on Saturdays," said Genna.

"Yes, we're a small congregation of Ashkenazi Jews here in Worthing, and a rabbi comes over from Brighton to officiate. But why should that interest you?"

"We are more interested in your wartime activities, Mr. Steener. We understand that you sheltered some orphans from London."

Mr. Steener smiled and nodded.

"Was one of them named Ephraim Goldfeldt?" I asked.

"Ephraim! Of course, I remember him well. He was one of several children sent down from Norwood during the Blitz. As I recall, he was a special case."

"How so?" said Genna.

"He was more difficult to place with a family because of language difficulties, but also he was not an easy child."

"I know he couldn't speak English," I said.

"But since he spoke Yiddish, he stayed here with me. He had a difficult young life—his father died at the hands of the Nazis, and his mother and her family lived in Paris, so he didn't know what happened to them. But he wasn't hopeful. Indeed he was very resentful."

"What eventually happened to him? We heard he was adopted."

"Yes, later we also housed an American officer for a few weeks. And as luck would have it, he spoke Yiddish, too. This officer got on well with the boy, and when he left to return home, he took Ephraim back to America with him."

"When was that?" said Genna.

"At the end of the war in Europe, in 1945."

"Have you heard from him since then? Do you know where he lives?"

"Oh, yes," said Mr. Steener. "I received several postcards from him when he was still a child, but nothing recently."

"So, where does Ephraim live?"

"He wrote about how peaceful the countryside was, but he never mentioned a name."

"But there has to be a postmark," I said, a little exasperated. "Didn't you read it?"

Mr. Steener shook his head. "I'm sure I did, but I don't remember it. It wasn't a name I recognized. Let me see if I can still find one." With that Mr. Steener got to his feet and left the room.

"We're getting somewhere now," said Genna. "Maybe you will meet your half-brother soon."

"Who knows, maybe I will. At this point I really don't know how to feel about that. He could be the one who forced my mother into that ravine."

"You have to think positively, Tommy," she replied, as Mr. Steener walked back into the room.

"I found a couple," he said, as he handed them over. "The text is in Yiddish, but as you can see, the address is in English. The postmark on both of them is Tannersville, New York, wherever that is. I hope that is helpful to you."

"That's very helpful, Mr. Steener," said Genna. "Thank you very much." She turned to me. "I know Tannersville, it's a district in the town of Hunter; I've been there. It has a thriving Jewish community, and it's only about five miles west of Katterskill Falls."

"My mother's studio is in Hunter," I said, as calmly as I could. The possibility of Ephraim living so close gave me chills.

26

When Genna and I returned to the States, I needed time to absorb and comprehend everything I had learned. My voyage to Europe had confused and troubled me, especially Padrig's description of my mother's early life. No wonder she refused to discuss it and went out of her way to block those experiences from her memory.

But now I had to track down those who might still want to harm her twenty years later. Unfortunately, my original and most likely suspect, Ephraim, was still proving elusive.

We visited the synagogue in Tannersville, but the person we talked to wasn't willing to identify himself, was barely cordial, and insisted he knew nothing about a refugee from Europe named Ephraim Goldfeldt. No matter how much we pressed him, he professed not to know anyone who might help. I even described the young man wearing a yarmulke who had brought some boys from a camp into the studio. But he simply stared at me with a blank expression. This seemed awfully suspicious. What was he hiding?

We were, however, more successful with Fernand, thanks to Genna and her connections throughout New York State. It turned out he was a young lawyer living and working in Albany, and his hobby was indeed hiking and climbing.

We managed to find an address for his hiking club and signed up to receive their newsletters. These newsletters told us when and where the club would be hiking each weekend, where they would meet and who would lead. More often than not that leader would be Fernand Le Goff. Coincidentally the Saturday after I arrived back at Middlebury College to resume my studies, Fernand was leading a hike in the Green Mountains just six miles south of the school. When first I got in touch with Adriana, I asked if she could to meet me at the cemetery early that same morning.

"Of course," she said. "Where else could we possibly meet? What do you want to do?"

"I know," I said. "You've been on my mind for a while. Let's go out to breakfast and get to know each other."

* * * *

I stood beside the grave, nervously glancing at my watch every few seconds. How should I greet Adriana? More importantly how much should I tell her about my mission? After all, I was searching for a man who burned down our house and possibly ran my mother off the road and into a ravine.

He was dangerous. Was this the right time to begin a relationship? Would I put Adriana in danger?

But Frank had met my mother on a dark night in the middle of the English Channel a few months into a merciless world war. He was only a year older than I am now, and he didn't have just one man trying to kill him—he had all of Hitler's efficient armed forces, and that didn't stop him for a second. He jumped in without hesitation, and it was lucky for me that he did.

Perhaps I was over-thinking this. After all, I wasn't going to ask Adriana to marry me; I was simply taking her out to breakfast.

But when I heard a voice calling my name, all my doubts and anxieties came flooding back—would she like me? What would I do if she didn't?

"Tommy, am I late? I'm so sorry. I didn't mean to be."

Adriana walked up to me holding out her hands. I took them in mine, hoping my relief didn't show on my face.

"You're even lovelier than I remember," I said, my cheeks growing warm. "But no, you're not late; I got here thirty minutes early. I'm ashamed to admit it, but I woke up at five and couldn't get back to sleep."

"I know what you mean. I was nervous coming here myself."

"Are you hungry? Because I'd like to take you to an old inn in East Middlebury. I'm told it serves a nice weekend brunch."

"It's true we have a lot of catching up to do. But I don't have a car; how would we get there?"

"I'm using a friend's car right now, but I'll be buying one soon, if I can find something cheap," I said, as I took her hand. "I hope you're hungry."

And as I gazed at her warm smile, it seemed as if a heavy load had somehow lifted off my shoulders.

As we headed south out of Middlebury, the Green Mountains on our left, I realized I needed to focus more on finding Fernand than starting a relationship.

Adriana brought me back from my dark thoughts by asking me about my voyage to France, especially the things I learned about my mother.

"It must have been an exciting trip," she said, "but did you learn anything that would help you find her killer?"

"I did," I replied. "But before I tell you what I found, I need to research something. When we get to the restaurant, I promise I'll tell you the whole story."

About six miles south of town, I saw a sign for Lake Dunmore and turned off the highway. Two miles later the road started to curl around the lake, and I pulled into a parking lot, parking at the far end.

"What are we doing here?" said Adriana suspiciously, as she took in the empty lot.

"There's a group of hikers meeting here soon, and I want to observe them. It's run by a hiking club based in Albany I'm thinking of joining. It's all part of my investigation. Try to be patient; I'll tell you all about it when we get to the restaurant."

Adriana regarded me with a little frown.

"Don't worry," I said. "This won't take long."

Adriana laughed then. "I'm not worried. I thought you were going to kiss me."

Before I could take her up on her invitation, cars with New York license plates started to pull into the parking lot, and young men and women dressed for a hike gathered together.

When a tall, good-looking man arrived in a two-toned Chevy, the group gathered around him, obviously their leader. He spoke to them quietly for several minutes and then with a wave, he led them across the parking lot and up through a rocky path, out of our sight.

"Who is that?" whispered Adriana.

"His name is Fernand Le Goff, and he is, as the police would say, 'a person of interest.' He belongs to a family who sheltered my mother and my birth father and then paid a terrible price for that shelter after she escaped to England. He's actually one of two people I'm interested in."

"He seems a little young to have known your mother in France."

"He is, but they lived on the same farm when he was a little boy."

"And the other guy? Is it a guy?"

"Yes, it's a guy, and strangely enough, he might be my half-brother. But I'm getting ahead of myself; I'll tell you the whole story when we get to the Inn."

"I can't wait." Adriana reached over and squeezed my hand. "This would make an amazing book. Have you ever thought of that?"

"I have, but first I have to write the last chapter. If you're willing, I hope we can write it together."

Adriana said nothing; she simply leaned toward me. There was nothing else I could or wanted to do, so I kissed her.

I was still smiling when we reached the Inn in East Middlebury.

* * * *

"That's an amazing story. Your poor mother; how did she survive all that? And all those people you met—what a cast of characters—especially Padrig and his fishing partner, Yann!"

We had been sitting at our table for over two hours, and up to that moment, Adriana had hardly spoken a word.

"You're right; it's an amazing story. But it's also potentially dangerous, and I'm still wondering whether you should get involved," I replied.

Adriana reached for the coffee pot and refilled our cups. "I can help you, and what's more, I *want* to help you. What's the next move?"

"I think it would unnerve Fernand to no end if I joined the hiking club."

"If he's the guilty party, then yes, it would. But do you think it would unnerve him enough to push you off a cliff?"

"I hadn't thought of that," I said.

"Then I should join, too. We could watch each other's backs."

27

Adriana and I became inseparable after that. We did join the hiking club but weren't able to participate in any hikes until their next hike in Vermont, along a ten-mile section of Vermont's Long Trail that follows the Green Mountains from Massachusetts to the Canadian border. Our day would end just east of Rutland in the parking lot of the Pico ski area, where a van would take us back to our starting point and our cars.

When we pulled into the parking lot that was our assigned meeting place, the lack of people there confirmed that we were early. There were, however, two young women dressed in clothes suitable for a day's hike leaning against a battered World War II army surplus Jeep.

"Hello," I said, as we approached them. "Are you members of the hiking club?"

"Yes, we are," said the younger, prettier girl. "I'm Mac and this is Mickie. We're charter members, actually. Welcome aboard."

We explained who we were and where we were from and engaged in small talk while we waited for the other hikers.

"So," said Adriana. "How did the club get started?"

"Funnily enough, it began over a love of Gaelic languages," said Mac. "My brother, who was a lot older than me and was known as Big Mac—I'm Little Mac—was born on the Hebrides Islands of north-western Scotland. In the Hebrides they speak Scottish Gaelic.

"Anyway, he met this Frenchman at his work who also spoke a form of Gaelic; he called it Brezhoneg or Breton, and they bonded as they discussed the differences and similarities of the two languages. But then, when they both expressed a love of hiking, too...." Mac raised her arms and shrugged her shoulders as a sign of inevitability.

"A Frenchman, you say," I said. "My parents were French, and I was over in Brittany a few weeks ago. What is his name?"

"His name is Fernand Le Goff, and he looks and sounds like a gigolo," said Mickie, disparagingly.

"Don't listen to Mickie; Fernand is a great guy," said Mac. "Oh, here he is now," she continued, as a cream and green 1955 Chevrolet Bel Air pulled into the parking lot. "Fernand, come over and meet some new hikers."

Fernand's eyebrows lifted slightly when I introduced myself, and he looked surprised when I suggested that we may have met before.

"Didn't you come to my mother's art studio in the Catskills once? I seem to remember your face."

"No, it wasn't me," he replied quickly. "Who is your lovely hiking partner?"

Did he change the subject on purpose, or was I simply paranoid?

Fernand flipped immediately into what Mickie had described earlier as 'gigolo' mode when I introduced Adriana. He shook her hand warmly and welcomed her to the club, his continental accent wrapped carefully around every word.

He made my feeble attempts at sophisticated conversation seem like the grunts and stammers of a country boy. Although I was pleased that Adriana didn't seem overly impressed.

So much for you, Frenchie boy.

* * * *

When we stopped for lunch, Fernand, Mac, and Mickie joined us on our rock, and Fernand spoke to me in French.

"Do you have your mother's artistic talent, Tommy?"

"Not really," I replied in English. "It seems I'm more like my birth father. In fact, I would like to continue one of his projects one day."

"And what is that?" he asked.

Adriana also turned toward me expectantly. "What could that be, Tommy?" she asked.

"Jean-Pierre originally went to Brittany to collaborate with Padrig the Raconteur on a book of Breton tales and legends. I would love to renew that project. It would marry nicely with a biography of my mother that I'm contemplating writing."

"You are thinking of writing a biography of Jacqueline?" said Fernand dismissively. "Who would buy the story of an unknown artist?"

"If she is unknown now, she won't be soon. An art appraiser is putting together an exhibition of my mother's paintings. She wants to move the exhibit from museum to museum around the country, and go to France, too, if she can arrange it. She wants me to write a biographical essay for the brochure. We believe my mother was not only a talented artist but a heroine of the Résistance, and we want the world to hear her story."

Fernand quickly changed the subject.

Had I already hit a nerve? Showcasing Jacqueline's life and work would also shine a spotlight on her death and make it more questionable, even though that wouldn't happen overnight.

Fernand, however, told us what to do if and when we encountered a bear, something, he said, that had happened to him several times since he had taken up hiking. He sounded sincere and caring. Was I being too suspicious?

This time I changed the subject. "Do you hike in the Green Mountains all the time, Fernand?"

"Here or in the Adirondacks, mostly, although we occasionally do the Catskill Mountains. The Catskills were Big Mac's territory. He used to lead the hikes there. I don't know much about them."

* * * *

After the hike, and after saying goodbye to Fernand, Mac, and Mickie, Adriana and I drove back to campus.

"Are you really thinking of writing a book about your mother?" Adriana asked. "Or was that just a ruse to rattle Fernand?"

"Do you think it worked?" I said with a smile. "For now, it's just an essay for the exhibition brochure, but if her paintings are well received, I might turn it into a book. If Fernand is guilty, putting Jacqueline's story front and center in the public eye would unnerve him completely, don't you think?"

When we reached my room, Adriana threw herself on my rickety bunk-bed.

"I'm beat," she said.

"You were talking to Mac practically the entire hike," I said. "That uses up a lot of energy. Did you learn anything interesting?"

"Well, it was mostly just family history; she evidently idolized her brother Keith, as he was known in the family. When war broke out in '39, he even went back to Scotland and joined the Seaforth Highlanders, the regiment that wears the family tartan. He transferred to an American regiment later in the war, however, so he could take advantage of the GI bill and go to law school.

"He died from a fall hiking in the Adirondacks last winter. Mickie was his girlfriend. She doesn't seem to think much of Fernand, although I got the feeling that Mac, whose name is Janet, is secretly in love with the guy. She denies it, though."

"Wow, you learned a lot," I said.

"That's not all. That Jeep they were driving? That belonged to Mac's brother. He left it to the hiking club."

"But is there something else bothering you?" I asked, after studying Adriana's face.

"It's this Genna lady. She sounds like a super woman, and she obviously means a lot to you."

"Of course she does. I owe her everything. But she's not coming out of this empty handed. My mother's paintings could be worth a lot of money, and I intend to pay her for everything she's done. Without her I'd be nothing but one of Frank's construction workers."

"How old is Genna? Were she and you ever, um…"

I laughed and leaned over to kiss her.

"Genna is my mother's age and happily married to a successful writer," I said. "Anyway, you are the only good thing that's happened to me in the last two years. You're gorgeous and you're wonderful." I ducked my head. "And now I'm blushing again."

With that, she lifted her eyes to the heavens, but kissed me anyway.

28

Our next hike was scheduled for the Catskills. We would climb a mountain only fifteen miles from where my mother died, and less than ten miles from Tannersville, the village from where Ephraim sent his postcards to Mr. Steener. We stopped at a coffee shop there for breakfast. It was almost nine and we'd already been on the road for three hours.

"This is going to be a long day," said Adriana, as we slipped into a booth by the window. "How long is the hike?"

"Five hours, I think; that's about average for this club."

"And we still have to find the starting point. We won't be back in Vermont until midnight. Couldn't Fernand have picked a closer mountain?"

I laughed. "Remember that the club is based in Albany, not the Green Mountains. But we don't have to go back to Vermont; we can stay at my mother's old studio. There's a pull-out couch we can use, and we can drive back to Vermont in the morning."

"Oh, wow," she said. "Are any of her paintings still there?"

"No, Genna has them in storage at her home in Saugerties. And that's where they'll stay until the first exhibition."

I explained that Genna was in discussions with Middlebury College for a showing at their museum in the spring. "I got a letter from her. She's coming up to Middlebury to talk to the museum curator."

At that moment a waitress came by with a coffee pot.

"Yes, please," I said, pushing my cup toward her. I waited until she finished pouring before I said, "Excuse me, miss, but are you from around here?"

"Pretty much," she said. "What d'you wanna know?"

"I'm looking for a Jewish boy who was brought here from England after the war."

The waitress shook her head. "The Jewish community here keep themselves to themselves. You won't get much from them unless they know you."

"I know," I said, "I was at the synagogue in Tannersville and the guy I spoke to wasn't willing to tell me anything."

"Well, you might try the synagogue in Hunter."

"Thank you," I said, but to Adriana I added, "When Genna and I were at the Tannersville synagogue, I should have told them he was my half-brother. We might have gotten better results." I glanced at the clock. "We'd better get going. We're going to be late."

* * * *

"Watch your step, everybody, and don't fall behind." With that suggestion, Fernand wished us all a pleasant hike and led the way along the surprisingly mellow first section of the trail.

After about two miles we came to a trail junction, and Fernand called us all together again. "We are roughly two thirds up the mountain, folks, but from now on we will be hiking the Devil's Path. The Devil's Path is one of the most difficult and dangerous hiking trails in the Catskills, indeed the world, and there is usually at least one death each year—either from a fall or a heart attack. So, my friends, if you are not in good shape or you're afraid of heights, I strongly advise you to turn back. The Devil's Path is not for you.

"I'm going to take a five minute break here, and then am going to continue to the summit. You decide what you want to do." With that, Fernand removed his backpack, found himself a rock and pulled out his water bottle.

He was immediately surrounded by several hikers with questions. One couple, roughly my age and probably also college students, talked of turning back and just wanted confirmation that this was the right thing to do.

Fernand was happy to oblige. "For the next two hours we'll be ascending or descending very steep terrain. You'll hang onto rocks, roots and shrubs, climb around huge boulders and patches of mud, and even wade through running water. Trust me when I tell you; if you have doubts, turn back. You'll be glad you did."

After listening to this last piece of advice, I took Adriana's hand and led her to a fallen tree on the other side of the clearing. She asked what was bothering me.

"It's Fernand," I said. "I see him leading hikes and hear him dispensing trail advice to the other hikers. It's obvious he's been hiking these Catskill trails for years. Yet he told me he knew practically nothing about the region."

"So now he isn't simply a person of interest," said Adriana. "He's a suspect. We have to be more careful. We don't want to give him the opportunity to push you off the mountain. Maybe we should turn back, too. Let's face it; he seems to know the trail like the back of his hand. If he did push us off a cliff, we would never see it coming."

"What are you two plotting over there, with your heads so close together? You must be up to something." Fernand was back on his feet and pulling on his backpack. "Come, *mes amis*, it is time to attack the Devil's Path."

"I was telling Adriana that there's going to be a retrospective of my mother's artwork at our college in the spring. Isn't that wonderful?"

"Jacqueline's paintings were good," he replied. "I remember the one at Chantal's house. But are they good enough for an exhibition?"

"Well, let's leave that to the art experts. I'll stick to writing, and you stick to hiking and climbing, which you're really good at. I'm impressed."

Fernand smiled at the compliment and turned his attention to his group. "Okay, who is going to continue with this hike?"

The young couple shook their heads. "No, we're gonna call it a day. You all enjoy yourselves; be careful, but enjoy. We'll see you in a few weeks."

In all, five hikers decided not to continue, which left a group of seven: Fernand, and of course Mac and Mickie, a middle-aged man named Jeff and his much younger girlfriend, Rosie, and Adriana and me.

Before we started up the very steep trail, Jeff insisted on shaking hands with everyone and making sure we all knew everyone's name, especially that of his beautiful girlfriend.

I noticed that both Fernand and Rosie smiled broadly at each other when they shook hands, and I wondered if Jeff's pride in her wouldn't backfire. Fernand's darkly handsome features and sexy French accent would be hard to resist. And of course, Rosie couldn't possibly know that he was a murder suspect.

Almost immediately we were confronted by an almost-sheer rock face of about twenty-five feet, with a tree that grew right beside it. Fernand showed us the preferred route up, which was basically right between the tree and the face of the rocks, and pointed out the foot holds and hand holds we could use.

"I am going up and I would like one other hiker to come with me. At the top this other hiker will lower a rope and pull up all your backpacks, and I will give advice and assistance to you all as you ascend one at a time." Fernand turned to me. "Will you follow me up, Tommy?"

I nodded and removed my pack.

The rest watched as we climbed the rock face—I followed Fernand and had very little trouble.

At the top, I called down to the others: "Here's the rope, folks. Tie on the first bag."

Mickie tied her bag onto the rope, and I pulled it up. She then climbed the rock face, slipping and sliding as she went. But as Fernand pulled her over the top, Rosie said she'd seen enough and was going back.

I looked at Jeff, not sure what to expect, but he simply shook his head and then stepped back into the clearing and called up to Fernand.

"Rosie wants to turn back, Fernand, and I'm going with her. Sorry about that. Have a nice day."

Mac, who had just tied her bag onto the rope, simply waved goodbye and climbed up around the tree.

"I can't even watch her," said Rosie, calling up to us as she pulled on her backpack. "I can't imagine what I was thinking when I agreed to continue. I hope that Jeff isn't too disappointed with me."

She glanced at Jeff, who looked more relieved than disappointed.

"I don't think you have a problem, Rosie," said Adriana. "Maybe we'll see you on another hike."

Rosie and Jeff gave her a quick hug and turned back along the trail.

Ten minutes later, Fernand pulled Adriana over the cliff face, and we continued up to the peak. There were very few stretches where we could simply walk, and in many sections we pulled ourselves up by exposed tree roots and other hand holds.

It was easy to understand why it was called The Devil's Path.

At the mountain's summit the trail leveled off, although we were surrounded by trees that blocked any views. Fernand, however, promised that views were just down the trail.

"Have patience," he said.

"So, Fernand," said Mac, who was gasping for breath. "It's all downhill from here, right?"

"That's true," he replied. "But that doesn't mean that it's going to get easier. Climbing down a cliff face can be more difficult than climbing up it."

Mac and Mickie looked at each other, looked back at Fernand, and shook their heads.

"Look at the bright side," said Fernand. "Lunch rock and some spectacular views are less than fifteen minutes away. Indeed, all the great views are on this side of the mountain. Follow me, my friends." And with that he pulled on his backpack and began down the track.

When we arrived at the flat rock that served as the traditional lunch area and viewing station, Fernand called us together. "We are at the Peak of Indian Head Mountain, and those two peaks to the right are Sugarloaf Mountain and Plateau Mountain. Those birds you see flying around are warblers who nest up around here. Enjoy your lunch."

Our mood lightened considerably as we consumed our sandwiches and sipped our water.

Fernand, who sat beside me, asked me in French if I was going back to France, but because Adriana was there, too, I replied in English.

"I haven't made any concrete plans, although I'll probably return in the summer; perhaps for a month."

"For a month?" said Fernand. "What are you going to do in Brittany for a whole month?"

"I plan on spending most of the time fishing with Padrig and Yann and working on an anthology of Breton tales and legends."

"Interesting," said Fernand. "Would you publish it in French or English?"

"Hopefully both, but I'm sure the French version would sell more. The English version would be more of a vanity project. I'd like to try to find my half-brother, too."

"Oh, yes, Ephraim; I remember him vaguely. How old would he be now?"

"I'm not sure—around thirty, I guess. His grandfather was a rabbi in Paris and hoped Ephraim would become one, too. I don't really know where to start, I don't know much about the religious side of being Jewish."

"Even though you are half-Jewish yourself?"

"That may be true, but I was raised Catholic by my mother and the man I thought was my father. I just want to meet Ephraim. Let's face it; during the war we escaped on the same boat, even if I was still in the womb."

"I guess that's true," said Fernand, as he got to his feet. "Okay, gang, let's tackle the descent."

It wasn't long before we arrived at an almost vertical fifty-foot cliff face.

"We have to climb down that?" said Mac, dubiously.

Fernand nodded. "This is the most difficult section, but there are lots of tree roots to hold on to. Why don't you come down with me, Mac? I'll keep you safe."

While Adriana, Mickie and I watched, Fernand and Mac negotiated the cliff together.

All in all they took about twenty minutes, and when they were at the bottom, Mac gave Fernand a hug and kiss and then gave us, looking down from the top, two thumbs up.

"Come on down," she called. "It's not so bad."

But when I glanced at Mickie, I could see she was not at all pleased. She began her descent muttering about the so-and-so French gigolo and how his hands had been all over Mac on the way down.

Nonetheless we made it down without any problem and began our descent down a narrow trail with a rock wall to our left and a row of white pine trees on our right. These trees were our only barrier to a hundred-foot cliff just beyond them that was, according Fernand, certain death.

Leading the way was Fernand, with Mac following her hero directly in his footsteps. Some fifteen feet behind them came Mickie, still muttering and still visibly upset. Adriana and I brought up the rear.

What happened next is still a blur in my mind, although I have tried to piece it together moment by moment many times—both for myself and as I related the incident to the local authorities, and especially to Deputy Perkins.

We were walking down the trail when Mickie slipped on a wet stone. She fell against the rocks to the left, wobbled for a second, and then overcompensated toward the right. She fell and slid toward two of the straggly pines that guarded the cliff. I was two or three steps ahead of Adriana and shouted a warning, then leapt toward her. The next thing I knew, the lower half of my body was caught by the small pine, and my chest and arms were half way over the edge as I still hung onto Mickie.

Then Fernand pushed past Adriana. But instead of pulling me back onto the path, he pushed me closer to the edge.

I heard a scream and Adriana pushed Fernand off me. He landed farther down the path, falling on his face. Adriana grabbed my legs and caught them against the tree to prevent me from sliding off the trail. Mac fell to her knees beside her and together, using strength I had no idea either of them possessed, they managed to drag first me and then Mickie back onto the path.

We all collapsed against the rock face, shaking and gathering ourselves. Mickie, her face devoid of color when she was finally pulled to safety, sat gasping for air, staring silently at the gap between the sparse conifers.

Fernand clambered back to his feet, dusted himself off, and turned toward us. He acted as if the entire incident was simply a foreseeable mishap, an everyday obstacle when climbing in the Catskills. He congratulated us on our combined efforts and told us to stay where we were until we were all ready to continue.

He made no mention of his own actions and behaved as though he had done absolutely nothing wrong. Indeed, when we arrived at our parking spot, he hugged and kissed both Mac and Mickie on the cheek, Gallic style, and sent them on their way with a cheerful wave.

By the time Fernand turned back toward Adriana and me, we had stowed our backpacks in our car and Adriana was already in the passenger seat. He walked toward me, a cautious smile already on his lips.

I was not sure what to do or what to say.

"That was quite a day," he began. "We were very lucky up there."

"Is that what you call it?" I replied, anger suddenly welling. "I'm not sure what to think. You were no help at all. You simply got in everybody's way. Call yourself a hike leader? I have a good mind to punch you in the face."

Fernand's mouth gaped open as he stepped back. "I was simply trying to help, and Adriana got the wrong impression of what I was doing."

"We'll see about that," I said.

I would report Fernand's actions to Deputy Perkins, but making Fernand aware of my suspicions now would not be very helpful. So when Adriana got back out of the car and attempted to smooth things over, I grudgingly allowed myself to be soothed.

We finally shook hands all around, got into our respective cars, and drove away.

29

Adriana and I went to the art studio that evening, and the next morning I got in touch with Deputy Perkins and told him of my suspicions.

"Are you sure?" he said, after I explained the connection between our two families. "You believe this man Le Goff harbors such a murderous hatred of you and your mother that he is willing to drop you over a cliff for something that happened twenty years ago? It's hardly likely; you weren't even born yet."

"I can't be certain, but I could feel his sister's hostility when I first visited her farm. It was chilling. And besides that, we don't really have any other suspects."

"Well, we don't actually know for sure that your mother's death was not an accident."

"That may be true, Deputy, but our house didn't burn down by itself."

* * * *

After agreeing with me that Fernand's actions warranted further investigation, Deputy Perkins signed off, and I didn't hear from him for a week or so. When he did get in touch with me, however, he was very positive about Fernand, both his standing in the legal community in Albany, and the fact that when the Sherriff interviewed him, he had an alibi for both the night of the fire and the night of my mother's death.

"We even checked his car, a '55 Chevy Bel Air," said Perkins. "It's in mint condition, and there's no sign of any scraping on the passenger's side and no sign of any repairs or touch up paint there, or anywhere else for that matter. I'm sure that you're mistaken, Tommy. But thank you for the tip; it was certainly worth checking out."

When I reluctantly relayed this information to Adriana, she was able to absorb it and believe it much easier than me.

"He seems like such a nice guy," she said. "I, for one, am glad he's no longer a suspect. You should apologize to him."

"Maybe," I replied. "But it sure felt like he was trying to push my legs away from that tree."

"Well I thought so too, but we must have been mistaken. However, if you still have doubts, why don't we socialize with him more? The more you talk to Fernand, the better you would get to know him and his real character."

I grudgingly agreed, although I made no immediate plans to send out any feelers. That could wait.

* * * *

If Fernand was a dead end, as he seemed to be, my mother's killer could only be Ephraim. The following Sunday we drove into Hunter and found that the town was indeed made up of two distinct villages, Hunter and Tannersville. And just as the waitress told us, each village had its own Jewish community. We also found that each one had its own separate post office, too, and although Ephraim's postcards were stamped Tannersville, New York, I had visited the wrong synagogue.

We found the Hunter synagogue and met with the rabbi. He was eager to help after I identified myself, but at first he was unable to recall a refugee named Ephraim Goldfeldt.

"There are many families that only come here during the summer," he said. "Perhaps your brother was only here in July and August. How old would he be now?"

"He would be about thirty now," I said. "But if this is any help, I'm pretty sure he was training to become a rabbi. And when he was in England, he was sheltered by a congregation of Ashkenazi Orthodox Jews."

"Wait a minute," said the Rabbi. "I do remember a boy who attended our summer camp for a couple of years. He was a handful at first, but he got better as his English improved. I don't recall his name, but my son might; he was a camp counselor around that time. Let me call him in."

After the rabbi made the introductions, he explained our dilemma to his son Aaron.

"Do you remember that boy?" he said.

"I think so," said Aaron. "There was a boy who was originally from Paris. I don't remember his name, but he had an enormous guilt complex."

"Did he ever tell you what was bothering him?" I said.

"Not at first, no, but I kept up a dialogue with him until he explained it to me. He said that he inadvertently caused his father to be captured by the Nazis, and the memory of that and his father's almost immediate death still haunted him. He also told me that he later learned his mother and grandparents died in the Nazi death camps. No child should ever go through life with those awful memories," Aaron continued, shaking his head sorrowfully.

"So, what did you do?"

"Well, Ephraim—is that what you said his name was?" I nodded, and he continued. "Ephraim had told me earlier that before the war he had begun rabbinical studies in Paris, but now he didn't feel worthy to continue with them. So I started working on that. I told him he couldn't change the past, but he could turn around his future and become the best he could be at whatever he desired to become—even a rabbi. And I worked on that idea with him for the rest of the summer."

"Have you kept in touch, Aaron? Do you know where he is now?"

He shook his head. "I'm afraid not, but I remember him saying that his adopted parents were an ex-army officer and his wife." Aaron narrowed his eyes. "Wait a minute, I think they lived in Allentown. I can't swear to it, but I believe that's it—Allentown, Pennsylvania."

"Thank you very much, gentlemen, you've been very helpful," I said as we shook hands, and Adriana and I drove back to my mother's studio.

We drove to Allentown the following day and did find a Jewish ex-army officer who sent his son to camp in Hunter, but the young man's name wasn't Ephraim and he certainly wasn't French.

"It seems like Ephraim has disappeared off the face of the earth," I said in despair, as we drove back to the Catskills.

"Maybe you've been wrong about this all along. Maybe it's someone other than Ephraim or Fernand. Speaking of Fernand, now would be a good time to call him and apologize," said Adriana, not willing to let it go. "It's no small thing to accuse somebody of murder, especially since the police have investigated him and found him not guilty."

"I never accused him to his face," I said. "And I'm still not totally convinced. It has to be one or the other of them. Who else would possibly want to kill my mother?"

"You could be right about that," said Adriana. "But we know where Fernand is, so let's call him and keep in touch. There's something I learned in philosophy class: Keep your friends close and your enemies closer. I'm not sure of the source, maybe Machiavelli, but it certainly answers your problem. If he's the one, he'll make a mistake sooner or later."

* * * *

While our efforts to find Ephraim continued to be elusive and frustrating, I did call Fernand. Before I knew it, we were back hiking together on relatively friendly terms, and Adriana was becoming especially friendly with Little Mac.

Mac's given name was Janet McLeod, and when she dressed for her job at a high-end travel agency in Albany, she was stunningly beautiful. She seemed, however, to prefer spending her evenings and weekends with Mickie, dressed in army fatigues and hiking boots. And that was what she was wearing when she arrived in her brother's Jeep at Fernand's house, when he invited us all to dinner.

"Do you take that thing to work?" I asked, referring to the beat-up Jeep. Mac and I were standing beside a picture window overlooking the road. Adriana was in the kitchen helping Fernand.

"It's not mine; my brother left it to the club. It just happens to be parked outside my apartment right now, and of course I wouldn't take it to work."

"So, anyone in the club can use it?" I asked.

"No," she said. "Only the few original members, and that's enough. It still gets beat up. We had to replace the front bumper last year. We still don't know how it got banged up."

"Interesting," I said. "Is Fernand on that list?"

She smiled and nodded, so I continued: "Have you been dating him long?"

"I wish, but he likes to keep it light. Although when I have somewhere to go that requires a date, he's a good guy to take, especially with that accent. He keeps the ladies enthralled with his stories. Fernand also calls me occasionally when he needs a companion. I once went with him to the Canadian Maritimes when he went there to meet with his uncle. That was quite a trip, I can tell you."

"You mean his Uncle Hervé?" I said, surprised.

"Yes, do you know him? He's a fishing-boat captain."

"I've never actually met him, but I've been to his house in France and met his wife. She's Fernand's mother's sister."

"What a small world!"

"So," I said, "how did you get there? By ferry?"

"Several ferries, actually. It took us two days, but eventually we arrived on a small island where everyone spoke French. It was an interesting experience."

"Really," I said. "But aren't there lots of people in Canada who speak French? It's their second language."

"Yeah, I guess so. Fernand's going there again in a couple of weeks."

"Are you going with him?"

"I don't think so. Don't get me wrong, it's a lovely island, but his uncle doesn't speak English, and I don't speak Breton, or even French, so it's a little boring for me."

We were interrupted by Adriana and Fernand bringing in the food. Dinner and the rest of the evening was devoted to the re-telling of hiking horror stories and other amusing incidents. We sat around after dinner gossiping until it was quite late. But we finally realized that Janet was patiently waiting for us to leave so she could discreetly accompany Fernand to bed.

When we got to our car, however, I pulled down the road a little and waited until the lights went out inside the house. Then we both crept back to inspect the Jeep. Sure enough, there were deep scrapes and dents on the front passenger side that were consistent with the Jeep being forced against another vehicle, pushing it off the road.

Adriana was horrified. "Oh my God," she said. "Now what do we do?"

"What can we do? I'll call Deputy Perkins first thing tomorrow morning, tell him what we found and give him Mac's address. Deputy Perkins told me she was Fernand's alibi for the two dates in question, so he'll be very interested in speaking with her again. I'm sure she'll change her tune if she's threatened with being an accomplice to murder. That should end it once and for all. Thank God!"

30

Deputy Perkins called me back two days later.

"You were right, Tommy," he said. "We impounded the Jeep and compared it to your mother's car. It could easily be the vehicle that forced her off that mountain road. We questioned Miss Mcleod again, and she admitted she became his alibi for a favor. Fernand told her he was home alone, but she doesn't know if he had the Jeep on the day your mother died. But…" He hesitated. "It was certainly enough evidence to bring him in for questioning."

"So what's the problem?" I asked, suddenly concerned.

"Le Goff seems to have disappeared."

"How could that have happened? Did Mac tip him off?"

"She swears she didn't, but I don't know exactly where her loyalties lie right now. Tell me, Tommy; in your dealings with Miss Mcleod, did you get any idea that she might be Fernand's accomplice in any of this?"

"No," I said. "I don't think so. I think they just had a casual relationship, and I stress the word casual. They didn't seem really serious, although Mac was maybe more serious than Fernand. Did she tell you of his upcoming trip?"

When he said no, I told Deputy Perkins about Fernand going to Newfoundland to meet his fishing-boat-captain uncle.

"He was supposed to go there again in a couple of weeks," I said. "And she told me he asked her to go with him. But if he's now on the run, perhaps he'll still go there and hide out until his uncle arrives. He could then go back to France on his fishing boat."

"Do you know exactly where they meet?"

"No, but Mac knows that, too. She went there with him once."

* * * *

After a couple days, Deputy Perkins called me to attend a meeting at the County Sheriff's office in Catskill. Mac was also there, but nobody knew where Fernand was. He had vanished.

The sheriff welcomed me into his office, and Deputy Perkins brought me up to date. "It seems that the island Miss Mcleod was referring to is actually a French overseas territory. It was ceded to France in the same treaty that made Québec part of the British Empire, and is used by the French for their deep-sea fishing activities. It's called St. Pierre, and it maintains a small army base and a police service known as the Gendarmerie."

"Did you find anything that points to him heading that way?"

"No, but it's worth checking out," he said. "Do you know Uncle Hervé's name, or the name of his boat?"

"His name is Riou, Hervé Riou, and he sails out of Vannes, located on France's north-western Atlantic coast. His boat is a deep-sea fishing trawler working primarily off Canada's Grand Banks. I'm sorry but I don't know the name of his boat."

"That really doesn't matter," said the Sherriff. "If he still plans to go there, he's going to get there as soon as possible. And we need to get there first. What we need from you, Mr. Kiernan, is for you to accompany Deputy Perkins to St. Pierre to act as an interpreter and also to help give us a positive identification of this fugitive as he steps off the ferry from Newfoundland. We've made the necessary arrangements with the Canadian and French Governments. We'll fly you to St. John's, Newfoundland, and a police launch will take you from there to St. Pierre."

* * * *

The next afternoon, Deputy Perkins and I stepped off the launch onto the dock at St. Pierre. The town hugged the waterfront and spread up a gentle hill. We checked in at our hotel, and when we were informed there was an Al Capone wing, we of course asked for a room there. Evidently Capone had used the island during the American prohibition as a warehouse for his bootleg booze.

And after we settled in, we walked to the ferry dock, which was located in a square with a huge statue dedicated to French sailors lost at sea. Everything about this island was connected and dedicated to that wild and unforgiving North Atlantic Ocean.

Wow, I thought, *I'm getting pretty good with words. Maybe I'll be a good writer someday. Wild and unforgiving ocean, not bad!*

We went into the building housing the ferry dock and checked the schedule. There was a ferry to Miquelon, the only other inhabited French island, and another one that went back and forth to Fortune, Newfoundland—one trip a day on weekdays arriving at noon, but with no service on Saturdays and Sundays. We looked at each other, shrugged and, since the ferry had long since arrived that day, settled in for the long haul.

We asked for directions to the Gendarmarie, and on arrival there I asked to speak to the Commandant. When he appeared from his office to greet us, a tall, erect gentleman with a thick dark mustache, we were happy to learn his English was very good. He ushered us into his office, introduced himself and asked what he could do for us on this tiny outpost.

"Weren't you expecting us?" said Deputy Perkins. "I understood that our visit had been sanctioned and arranged by our mutual superiors."

"Not to my knowledge, Deputy. But the Canadian Government usually deals with the army Commandant. In St. Pierre we are still under French martial law and have been since World War II."

"We are not from Canada, Commandant Lebrun. I am a Deputy Sheriff from New York state in the USA. We're hunting a French national named Fernand Le Goff, who was a lawyer living and working in New York state, but is now a murder suspect and fugitive."

Commandant Lebrun sighed and shook his head slowly. "I am confused," he said. "Why would a murder suspect come here to St. Pierre, even if he is French? There is nowhere to hide. The residents all know each other well, and a stranger would be noticed and picked out immediately."

Perkins turned to me. "Tommy, tell the Commandant everything you told me. Speak to him in French, so we can be sure there is no misunderstanding."

I spent the next half-hour explaining everything, starting from the day Fernand came to my mother's art studio and ending with the evening we found and inspected the damaged Jeep.

And when I was finished, his first question, which he asked in English, was if I knew the name of Uncle Hervé's boat.

"If this Hervé Riou has been to St. Pierre before, the harbor master will have a record of his visits and his purchases," he added.

"That I do not know, Commandant. I have never actually seen the boat or met her captain. I just know his wife and family. In any case, we assume Fernand will arrive on the island several days before his uncle does. We checked at the Hotel Robert; he has stayed there before, but if he made reservations there again, it would of course now be under an assumed name."

"If he has made reservations there, there would be no reason to arrest him at the ferry. We can pick him up whenever we want."

"Fernand Le Goff is a dangerous man, a wanted murderer," said Deputy Perkins. "And Tommy here is not simply the best person on this island to identify him; he's a victim of one of his murderous attacks. Once Le Goff sees him, he'll know he's trapped. In my opinion, the moment he steps off the ferry is our best chance to catch and subdue him without endangering innocent bystanders."

The Commandant reluctantly nodded his head. "I will see what I can do. Can you return here in the morning?"

"We can wait while you make a couple of telephone calls, Commandant. We've been chasing this man for days. Another few minutes won't matter."

The few minutes stretched into an hour, as the commandant asked permission to arrest Fernand. Once he received the go-ahead from his superiors in Paris, he then got into a prolonged argument about arrest protocol with the commanding officer of the army barracks.

Finally, it was agreed that the Gendarmerie would make the arrest, but a small detachment of soldiers would be present, too. The Commandant also reluctantly agreed to stay out of sight until the arrest was completed. They would meet the ferry every day for the next two weeks.

31

Three days later I stood to one side of the Ferry Terminus, watching as that day's passengers stepped ashore onto St. Pierre Island. There were maybe twenty people, including one with a week's growth of beard. Was he Fernand? I couldn't be sure, so I moved closer toward the gangplank.

Our eyes met briefly, and his face froze for a second. And then, as though he had been expecting a trap, he spun around quickly and shoved his way through his fellow passengers back up the gangplank and onto the ferry. He even knocked one loudly protesting man off the plank and into the water.

At the top of the gangplank, a burly crew member tried to block his path. Fernand pulled out a handgun, shot him point blank and pushed him aside. The seaman fell to the deck and lay still.

Fernand shouted at the few remaining passengers and herded them down into the passenger lounge. He slammed shut the bulkhead door behind him.

The report of Fernand's handgun echoed around the Ferry Terminus building, shocking everyone into a frozen silence. We all watched in open-mouthed disbelief right up to the final crash of the cabin door.

Seconds later the silence was broken by the squad of French soldiers, rifles at the ready. Their leader, a young lieutenant, stepped forward. "*Qu'est-ce qui s'est passé?* What happened?" he called in a loud, deep voice.

The sound roused us from our shock, and the gendarme sergeant quickly issued orders. He sent two men to guard the gangplank, two others to assist the unfortunate passenger in the water, and asked Deputy Perkins and me to help him get the remaining passengers out of the building and to safety.

We then consulted with the army lieutenant.

The military officer was not pleased. "So it seems," he said, his voice dripping with Gallic sarcasm, "that your simple arrest has evolved in the blink of an eye into an international hostage situation. Am I correct in this evaluation?" he added.

"I'm afraid so, Lieutenant," the gendarme sergeant said. "The other passengers tell me they are part of a tour group from Alberta Province, and the hostages are three middle-aged couples. They were to spend two nights on St. Pierre and then return to St John's. In any case, they are all Canadian citizens. The immediate question is: How do we free them without endangering their lives?"

"How do we free them without endangering anybody's life?" interjected Deputy Perkins. "That's the only possible course of action." He looked to the military officer for confirmation.

"And you are?" said the officer, as he looked questioningly at us both.

I introduced myself and quickly explained the situation, ending with a question of my own. "How do we communicate with him? There was a crewman on duty at the bottom of the gangplank. Where is he? He would know if there is a telephone in the lounge."

The crewman was quickly found and confirmed that there was an intercom in the snack bar. It was part of the inter-boat communication and we could call down from the bridge.

"You can get there by boarding the boat from the bow," he said.

The platoon of soldiers went to work with great efficiency and within the hour the boat was boarded, the gangplank removed, and the passengers' lounge surrounded by heavily armed soldiers.

By this time, the Gendarme commandant and a senior army officer were also both on the scene. They met with Deputy Perkins and me on the bridge.

"I understand that you know this man," said Colonel Joncourt, the assistant commander of the army barracks. "How can we get him to release his hostages? He must realize his position is hopeless. Do you believe he will surrender?"

"It's hard to say," I replied. "In any other situation, I found him to be easy to talk to and very reasonable. But I believe the memory of his murdered father and brothers consumes him. I don't think, however, that he means to harm those hostages."

"I hope not; the Canadian Government is very concerned. They want their citizens out of harm's way immediately. Even as we speak, there is a police launch on its way to St. Pierre." The colonel turned to the gendarme commander: "Do you have any ideas?"

"Why don't we establish contact with this man? Let us at least hear what he wants."

The colonel nodded and pressed the intercom.

"This is Colonel Joncourt of the St. Pierre Military Command calling Monsieur Fernand Le Goff. Can you hear me?"

"I hear you; what do you want?" Fernand's voice was quite distinct above the crackle of the intercom.

"I demand the safe return of your hostages, and that you surrender to us without any undue delay. Do you understand?"

"If you want your hostages back safely," said Fernand, "these are my demands: I want safe passage to the nearest airport and an airplane fully fueled ready to take me anywhere I wish to go."

"Unfortunately, Monsieur, a fully fueled airplane from the nearest airport could only get you to Canada or the United States. And there is a warrant for your arrest in both those countries."

"Surely not in Canada?"

"Monsieur Le Goff, your hostages are Canadian citizens. If you do not believe me, ask them yourself. Also, if you cast your eyes out onto the harbor waters, you will see a Canadian police launch has just arrived. You are now opposing the military might of two nations."

"Nevertheless, if I don't get that plane immediately, I'll begin shooting hostages. The first one will die in one hour."

I signaled to Colonel Joncourt. "May I speak to him?"

He shrugged his shoulders.

I called down to Fernand. "This is Tommy Kiernan, Fernand."

"So what, Tommy? Why are you here?"

I ignored the question and said instead: "I want to offer a prisoner exchange—me for the tourists."

"How would that benefit me?"

"To start with, it would remove Canada from the fast-growing list of countries who could arrest you. That is, if the crewman you shot is not Canadian."

Colonel Joncourt interjected: "The seaman is French and lives in St. Pierre. His wounds are not life-threatening."

"You hear that, Fernand? If you release the hostages, you would only be dealing with the French authorities in St. Pierre. Do we have a deal?"

The colonel spoke again: "Monsieur Le Goff, I am not in favor of this exchange, but the longer you hold those Canadian hostages, the worse it will be for you."

"And what about my airplane? Have you made any arrangements for that?"

"The Canadian government has asserted that if you harm any of their citizens, you will be shot on sight."

"Then let's make the exchange. I'll open the door at the top of the stairs, and when Tommy's in the lounge, I'll allow the hostages to leave. There must be no other personnel in sight. Is that clear?"

* * * *

As the last hostage filed past me on the stairs, he whispered, "Thank God for you, sir, whoever you are," and then he stepped out into the sunlight.

"Close the door and lock it, you brave, stupid fool," said Fernand. "If I don't get out of here and soon, my last act will be to blow your head off. Exactly the same as those Nazi pigs did to my father and brothers. Come, sit with me and have some whiskey. Let's drink together and discuss where our plane is going to take us."

I turned toward him and froze. "What are you doing?" I gasped.

Fernand was indeed sitting at the bar, a bottle of whiskey and two water tumblers beside him. But kneeling between his legs was a young woman. She sobbed as Fernand's hand twisted her hair. In his other hand he held a revolver.

"I needed some security. After all, I don't know if you're armed. And just in case you're wondering, she isn't Canadian, she's from Saint Pierre."

I bit my tongue. I had to make sure I didn't antagonize him. "I'm not armed. You can let her go," I said quietly.

"Let her go?" Fernand said, tugging at her hair. "She's my insurance."

"Insurance?" I said. "Insurance for what? You must realize your position is hopeless."

Fernand shook his head, dropped his gun onto his lap and picked up the whiskey bottle. "Do you want a drink or not?"

"Sure." I walked slowly toward him, holding out my hand.

"No, you don't." Fernand quickly snatched up his gun. "Go over there, and I'll slide your glass over to you." He indicated a stool that was six or seven feet to his left.

After I sat, he poured whiskey into two water glasses, slid one along the bar and picked up his revolver again. "What shall we drink to?"

"You have the gun. You decide."

"Tommy," he sneered, "the only decision I have to make is when I'm going to kill you."

"Will that make you happy?"

"It will settle the score once and for all. The Le Goff family will finally be avenged."

"Tell me, Fernand, when you walked into my mother's studio, were you looking for her?"

"No," he said. "But God sent me there to avenge my family."

"Well, then," I said, picking up my glass, "if that's what you believe, let's drink to that."

I lifted my glass in a toast, and Fernand let down his guard for a second. He dropped his gun to his lap, picked up his glass, and tossed his head back as he drank.

I leapt off the stool and punched the bottom of the tumbler as hard as I could. Fernand fell onto the floor screaming, blood streaming from his face.

He rolled over and rose to his knees as I clutched my hand. It felt broken.

I kicked him in the side of his head before he was able to get to his feet. He fell against the bar. The girl scrambled out of his way as he reached for the gun, but I managed to kick it away.

I tried to stomp on his hand and missed. He came at me and caught my jaw with a hard punch. I held up my arms to protect my face, and another punch hit my broken hand.

"You fuck!" I screamed in agony, cradling my hand.

Fernand threw himself at me, knocking me onto my back. The next thing I knew, he was on top of me, his hands around my throat, his blood dripping from his face.

"You bastard," he said, blood oozing from his mouth. "This is more satisfying, Tommy. I can watch your ugly face as I choke away your worthless life."

I struggled, but with the use of only one hand, I couldn't dislodge him. My sight dimmed... I was going to die.

The deafening sound of a gunshot filled the room. Fernand's body jerked, then slumped on top of me.

Gasping for breath, I wiped his blood from my eyes, pushed his body to the side and looked up.

Holding Fernand's revolver in both hands and still shaking with fear, his young and very brave hostage stood over us.

I slowly got to my feet and held open my arms. She lowered the gun and stepped into my embrace, blotting her tears on my shoulder.

I stared down at Fernand's body. What a waste, not only of his life, but that of my beautiful mother. I mourned not just her life, but the loss of her God-given talent.

Shouts from outside and pounding on the door finally roused us.

* * * *

Later, we sat in the Gendarme Commandant's office as Deputy Perkins called his office and reporting to the sheriff. He then handed the phone to me.

"Here, Tommy, someone wants to talk to you."

I picked up the phone expecting to hear the sheriff, but it was Adriana. She was almost sobbing as she spoke. "Oh my God, Tommy! I hear you were really brave, but also really stupid. Is that right?"

"Well, I was pretty stupid, that's for sure. But it worked out, thanks to a very brave young woman Fernand was holding hostage. How are you doing?"

"I'll be okay now that you're safe. But I heard you broke your hand. Are you okay?"

"It's definitely broken, but it will mend. Otherwise, I'm fine. What are you doing at the sheriff's office?"

"I stopped by to see when you were coming home. And the sheriff called me into his office and gave me his phone. When are you leaving?"

"I'll be back tomorrow. I can't wait to see you."

"Me, too. I love you."

32

Tommy Kiernan
Middlebury College, Vermont
October 1962

This weekend a retrospective of the life and work of Jacqueline de Bavière will open at the Art Museum on the College Campus at Middlebury. It is being presented by art historian Genna DeGraw, with a brochure containing a brief account of her life and death written by me, her only son, Tommy Kiernan. The exhibition will stay there for the remainder of the year before traveling to France, where it will be on display not only in Paris but in Vannes, Brittany, not far from where Jacqueline lived until her escape to England in July 1940.

During the time the exhibition is on display in Vannes, I have made arrangements to go to Kérity and meet with not only Fernand's family, but my half-brother Rabbi Ephraim Shapiro, who will be traveling from Paris, where he tends to the needs of a small congregation of orthodox Jews. It took me a while to find him, because he had changed last name to that of his adopted family and relocated back to Paris.

It will be our first meeting face to face. Through his communications to me over the last several months he told me that he remembers my mother and Padrig and fully appreciates everything they tried to do for him during those difficult and dangerous times. He also admits that his own rebellious nature may have caused, or at least contributed to, our father's death.

While we are in Kérity staying at the Auberge du Pont, of course, Adriana and I will host a dinner party to reunite Ephraim with Padrig, Yann, and possibly Jeanne-Marie, Annette, and Chantal, if they have recovered from the loss of their brother. Genna will also be there with her husband Daniel, and the theme of the evening will be the devastation and cruelty of war, and the long-lasting impact that stays with all who suffered through it.

I have thought about my mother's beautiful life and horrendous death many times—and her killer, too. How could Fernand have possibly believed that God wanted my mother dead? How could a pleasant and extremely intelligent man nurture this twisted and vengeful notion his entire life?

These questions will haunt me forever.

CPSIA information can be obtained
at www.ICGtesting.com
Printed in the USA
BVHW080847170619
551189BV00002B/243/P

9 781479 443055